The
Bee Hive

The Honey The Money The Sting

I H S A N A . R A J A B

THE BEE HIVE
THE HONEY THE MONEY THE STING

iUniverse books may be ordered through booksellers or by contacting:

iUniverse
1663 Liberty Drive
Bloomington, IN 47403
www.iuniverse.com
1-800-Authors (1-800-288-4677)

Because of the dynamic nature of the Internet, any web addresses or links contained in this book may have changed since publication and may no longer be valid. The views expressed in this work are solely those of the author and do not necessarily reflect the views of the publisher, and the publisher hereby disclaims any responsibility for them.

Any people depicted in stock imagery provided by Getty Images are models, and such images are being used for illustrative purposes only. Certain stock imagery © Getty Images.

ISBN: 978-1-5320-6521-7 (sc)
ISBN: 978-1-5320-6522-4 (e)

Print information available on the last page.

iUniverse rev. date: 08/13/2020

Acknowledgements

The elders say, "People enter our lives for a reason, a season, and a time." I humbly submit this page to give praise and thanks to those responsible for paving the way and providing the inspiration for the creation of this novel.

First, I give honor and glory to God Almighty, for without his providence none of this is ever possible.

Second, I give honor to my deceased father who was my best friend, mentor, and counsel; and in my opinion the world's greatest story teller.

I humbly wish to acknowledge my wife, Lauren, for providing me the space, peace of mind, and utmost encouragement for completing this novel and its publishing.

Last I appreciably give thanks and praise to Alta LeCompte. She is a multiple award winning publishing editor. She recognized my desire to write and she offered her patient, meticulous, professional skill set to accomplish this revised copy of The Beehive.

To all potential readers of this novel: it is my hope that you will enjoy it, as you navigate your journey through the Beehive.

Ihsan A. Rajab

Preface

Many of America's older cities were once manufacturing and industrial zones. They were beacons of hope for early immigrants from near and far who sought work for their families and better opportunities. Over a period of time a peculiar piece of real estate was formed between the old railroad lines and the industrial zones. This man-made haven established the divide between black and white neighborhoods, and the ideal location for crime and illegal activities.

The community initially seemed fruitful and safe. Over time, its industries changed, and many moved out, causing a negative impact to local economies. The absence of jobs and commerce created a void, which was replaced by criminal activities to satisfy lustful illegal appetites.

When I was very young I learned from my father and uncles about such a neighborhood in the Northeastern city where I was raised.

I remember their talk of prison life, and my favorite uncle's assertion that the criminal acts committed in the neighborhood where vice thrived bore much different results in prison for a Negro than a white person who committed the same crimes. I pondered that information for years.

Much later, I learned about the impact of the prison-industrial complex, where prisoners - an overwhelming number of whom are black - face a manipulation toward non-citizenship that is parallel to being a slave. I realized prison labor is akin to picking cotton.

I wrote *The Beehive* because I continue to mourn the degradation of our once-vibrant cities and de-humanization of their promising young men. This story will take you inside of a city that fosters crime and a maximum-security prison where prisoners pay their debt to society, the payment of which leaves our nation morally bankrupt.

The story focuses on a fictional character, Charles Jesus Sinclair, a young man who was tempted by the glamour of the city's center of vice but learned how to navigate a path to personal success and become an inspiration to others and a force for positive change in the old neighborhood and beyond.

I have written this story for you.

Ihsan Rajab

The Bee Hive

The Honey

The Money

The Sting

A Fictional Novel by

Ihsan A. Rajab

1

THE
HONEY

"How Sweet it is!"

CHAPTER 1

Into the world

The month of October is perhaps the most pivotal of all seasons representing change. It is without doubt the signature month that spells out the ending of pleasures and joys of summer life and the beginning slow process of death in a winter that is sure to come. The warm and inviting hues of red, orange, and soft gold are somewhat deceptive as they fall gently to Earth, and then wither toward a multi-clustering of cold death.

The cool temperatures lure an inviting, renewed air quality to the lungs, and welcome relief from the humidity, pollens, dew densities, and sweating of sizzling summer's heat. In a word, October reflects the seasonal cycles of our lives. The Earth and all its creatures exhale a sigh of gladness for the change that only fall weather can bring; if only for a little while.

Our lives are a mirror image of the seasonal change that occurs in nature.

At one point in time, men and women come together for complementary love; and within that procreation process one seed is planted, nurtured, and developed. This coming together begins our personal and seasonal journeys of what we interpret as our life.

Within this fall period of change, Charles Jesus Sinclair came into this world.

He was born on the dubious date of October 31, Halloween 1955. It was in the midst of a fierce rain storm, a colder than usual night. From the very beginning his life was shrouded by challenges and events that would remain attached to him for life.

His first eventful challenge occurred while he was still in the womb of his mother.

His story begins with a hurried, last minute arrival to a segregated

Negro hospital for an emergency delivery. This area of the hospital was quite a distance from the maternity and delivery section, dimly lit and poorly staffed. There were lines of buckets lined throughout to hold back the soaking rain that poured in from a busted and torn roof.

The constant sound of loud, anxious voices throughout that crowded space would suggest a chaotic environment, and yet one of a daily managed routine.

As time elapsed and stifling labor pains increased, Mrs. Anna Freda Diaz Sinclair at last bore witness to giving a breeched birth to her first and only male child.

The staff attendants for this hurried delivery propped her up on the nearest gurney as she wailed, moaned, and cried out at the sight of his tiny feet slowly emerging from her exhausted womb. Within moments of this notice, she began to faint from her ordeal, and with short panted breath, right before she passed out, she uttered "Mi Dios, mi Dios; my God, my God."

The nurses who were gathering nearby and waiting for the doctors' arrival began to realize that the time was now or never. They collectively agreed that they would somehow have to manage to get the baby safely aboard from the mother. This miraculous feat was never recorded, but some would say that the Almighty guiding hands of God assisted toward accomplishing this task, feet first and all.

There was an angel present among the crew on that stormy night.

Mama-Wanda, who had received her training from her Jamaican ancestors, had for decades been the legendary midwife within the Negro community. She had arrived at the hospital accompanying an old friend who within the past hour had survived a serious car accident.

While the hospital staff was aghast watching the breeched birth, Wanda sprang into action, taking control, barking orders in her native tongue with the precision of an army sergeant, directing anyone else toward whatever she needed. In a short time one of the assisting nurses who participated in this small miracle raised her arms toward the heavens, shouting, "Halleluiah. It's a boy, a bubbling, beautiful, brown baby boy. Yes sir, with 10 fingers, 10 toes, and a head full of black, curly hair."

The nurses and aides were beaming and collectively sighed with relief as the proud new mother lay exhausted and unconscious atop the messy gurney, now splattered with fresh blood and afterbirth.

At last the ordeal was over, and both mother and child were being wheeled toward an awaiting bed in the maternity ward.

As the two of them were comfortably joined together, with mother dozing in and out, there appeared a wry smile upon the baby's round, half-Cuban face.

The miracle child was peering at his mother with equal curiosity, yet free from the norm of wailing and that accompanies most newborns.

When Anna awoke the 9-pound infant seemed to be smiling right at her. He didn't begin crying until much later; and that was for silky-smooth milk from her blossoming, plump breast. She gently placed his naked body upon her breast and he frantically suckled, receiving the love and nourishment.

Meanwhile as mother and baby boy began a tranquil night of loving, bonding, and cuddling at Carver General Hospital, an absent dad was on his third round of Hennessey at Dee Dee's Lounge. The overall stress and doubt had taken its toll upon the disabled highly decorated veteran earlier that night, until he openly and willing surrendered to the fact that the final hours of pregnancy had become too much for him to bear. At last he delighted in a nervous, selfish scheme for escape and relief at Dee Dee's.

Upon entering to the infamous lounge, Carnell Sinclair received his usual upbeat greetings and cheers from the regulars. He was always welcomed and felt quite at home, even when an occasional fight would break out or the police would hassle and frisk some of the notables as a mask for retrieving their weekly protection payoff from the bar.

The sultry, smooth sounds echoing from the jukebox seemed to soothe his nerves as Nat King Cole intoned his hit tune, "Misty" in the way that only he could do. Strangely enough, the lounge wasn't crowded this particular evening, and that suited Carnell just fine. His desire was to unwind a bit, anticipating the weather would calm down and he would proceed to Carver General Hospital.

The atmosphere at Dee Dee's was enticing and more relaxing than the other neighboring watering holes, primarily because Dee Dee's husband, Artie, was a former welter-weight boxing champion. Artie didn't take any shit from anyone, including the hustlers, pimps, con-men and the tantalizing strolling whores. Denise, Artie's wife, was a former highly paid fashion model and was known to carry a pearl handled .45 caliber handgun, which she used on more than one occasion. Dee Dee's Lounge was a comforting place for Carnell to park his butt and relax his mind on this stormy October night; and he was exceedingly happy to be welcomed at his second home.

"What's up, my main man?" bellowed Jake, the tall, bearded bartender. "When is the baby due?"

I don't know," replied the weary, soon-to-be dad. "It may be here already. Give me a drink; I sure could use a cold one."

"Coming right up," said Jake as he reached for the chilled bottled of cognac.

"I couldn't stand it any longer; I put her in a cab and told her I'd be right behind her."

"I know what that feels like," said a nearby patron perched on a bar stool. I've got five and missed every one of them coming into this world."

"How come?" someone sitting at a table yelled out. "Because I just couldn't handle watching my pussy being destroyed by those big heads coming through it; it's intimidating."

Everyone laughed aloud, shaking their heads and pointing at Carnell. He raised his glass in salute and shouted, "Amen my brothers, amen."

After a few more drinks, joking, and small talk, Jake the barkeep glanced up at the clock on the wall and suggested that perhaps it was time for Carnell to get going to the hospital to see about his wife.

Two hours had elapsed and by now Carnell was feeling a little tipsy and anxious to learn if it was a boy or girl.

"I'll call you a cab," said Jake, "and you can forget the tab because it's on me." Big C, which was Carnell's nickname - not because of his size but because of his heart - stood up, adjusted his hat and jacket, and stumbled toward the men's room, eager to release an overdue piss.

"Thanks Jake, I hope it's a boy, but I won't be disappointed if it's a girl. I'll call you later and give you the news.

"Wow," Carnell continued, I 'm going to be a father, for the first time after all I've been through; I just can't believe it. Praise the lord.

"Dear God, I pray that my Anna and new child are happy, healthy, and safe."

As Carnell tipped his hat, checked his clothing and proudly strolled toward the door he noticed the rain and wind were calmly slowing down and the yellow cab was waiting at the curb. He gently pushed through the swinging doors turned his head towards the heavens and prayed, "Thank you, Lord. Please guide me to the loving arms of my new family.

"Amen."

It was 8:45 Saturday evening, when Big C pulled in front of the old two-story building of Carver General Hospital. The new father had no idea that his baby boy was already three hours old.

He sighed, took a deeper breath, approached the elevator, and then patiently waited for the ride to the maternity ward. Exiting at the second floor, he gingerly walked to the information desk, nervously introduced himself, and inquired about his wife's condition. The clerk, looking up with a smile, replied, "The mother and newborn boy are doing just fine."

Hearing this good news for the first time caused his knees to buckle, but it calmed his nerves and warmed his heart. He was so excited that he could hardly utter a word.

He finally stammered, "Where is he? Can I see my boy?"

The clerk, peering at him underneath her glasses, just smiled and said, "Follow me and I'll show him to you through the nursery window."

As he slowly approached the window he was beaming with a smile wide enough to have blocked out the sun.

The nursing attendant brought the baby toward the window, allowing Big C to take a long, investigating look. After a few minutes, he softly asked her through the speaker at the window, "Where is Anna, my wife?"

The courteous nurse replied, "She is resting peacefully in room 215."

Carnell quickened his steps in the direction to his worn-out wife, gushing with pride and heart's desire to embrace her with big hugs and long soft kisses. He was so excited touching the door that he quickly swung it open with a crash, which surprised the occupants of room 215.

"Hi honey," he said, grinning like the cat that just ate the canary. "How are you, my love, how you doing?"

With tears swelling from her beautiful, honey brown eyes, she reached for him and said, "Hey baby, I'm fine - just tired."

She was noticing the boyish look upon Carnell's face, and remembering the first time she ever saw that look and how much she loved it.

Leaning into her ear he whispered, "I just saw the baby, and it's a boy!"

"Yes honey!" Anna nodded, as though she didn't know.

"I gave you an 8-pound, 10-ounce love child."

Big C proclaimed immediately, "Thank God."

He wasn't a religious man; he didn't belong to any particular church or congregation, but he definitely believed in the One Almighty God. In this moment he was specifically thankful for the blessings of his wife and first child.

He embraced Anna's half naked, tender body with a strong bear hug, kissing her about the face, lips, and forehead.

"Careful honey," she sighed, "I'm still a little sore and my mouth is dry. Can you get me a glass of ice water?"

"Sure honey, anything you want, I'll get it."

He grasped the pitcher sitting on the small table near the bed and poured his glowing wife a tall glass.

She slowly sipped the water as if it was wine.

He paused and, after a long look, recognized the beautiful aura that shone like a halo about Anna's entire body. He was thinking to himself that angels of love, tenderness, and mercy were embracing his wife.

Carnell continued to stare but didn't want to interrupt this precious moment that only loving hearts could capture. Unable to contain himself any longer, he blurted out, "I am so proud of you."

That big grin of his, growing with each word, he continued, "I love you and you mean the whole world to me. I can't wait to tell the world about my two joys."

Suddenly, with tears flowing from his eyes and that infectious smile still present he softly said, "You gave me a son!"

The nurse brought in the baby for feeding and to check on the proud new parents. She left shortly thereafter, leaving them for some needed privacy, but said she would return after a while.

The three of them sat smiling with the full contentment and confidence that they were now a complete family. Sitting there in that small room was a picture-perfect moment of love and joy.

After the nursing time, Carnell held the baby with one arm while his wife snuggled ever closer. He was rotating his loving glances, first at the baby and then at Anna, when he asked the question, "What should we name him?"

She smiled and politely said with her Spanish accent, "Charles. After all that is your middle name, and now he is in the middle of both you and I."

The new dad smiled as he let her words sink in, and then replied, "Charles Jesus Sinclair, welcome to your new world, my son."

He gently full-kissed his wife on the lips, then whispered,

"You, too, honey, "You too!"

CHAPTER 2

Welcome home

Anna and Carnell were a happy and beloved couple of the neighborhood; they were respected by all and envied by most. Their good news spread quickly throughout the entire neighborhood and within three days the new family, nestled comfortably at home, received well-wishers and gifts for the new member of their community. The varied cast of characters from the Third Ward area was well represented as they each came to show their respect, offer prayers, and give gifts to its newest member.

Carnell was relaxing sitting in his favorite lounge chair when the doorbell rang once again to receive the next visitors.

Anna had managed to have one of her relatives send a box of Cuban cigars for this blessed occasion. She arranged them neatly on the table nearby within reach of Carnell's big hands. He agreed to only pass them out to the most esteemed members of the neighborhood or the ones he truly respected.

One by one the smiling, curious, and nosey neighbors entered their home to pay their respects to the new arrival. The parade of high and low life was on full display, morning, noon, and well into the night. The main notables were the flashy ministers from the nearby AME church, the owners from Dee Dee's Lounge, and even Bootsy the kingpin of hustlers and pimps and his money rival Madame Butterfly McQueen. These two gangsters brought baby clothes, money, and home-cooked meals that they had convinced local retailers to donate.

The Third Ward was a diverse community of good and bad characters with a range of moral codes, views, and agendas. Despite their petty differences, their beloved couple's new baby became the catalyst for badly needed unity.

One of the least likely characters to pay homage was Miss Sally Andrews, whose nickname was Sally from the Alley. She was the unfortunate vagabond who managed to build a shelter from an abandoned warehouse for her production of illegal homemade moonshine.

Rumors concerning Sally would change according to who was telling her story. The most popular story is that she was once a smart, pretty college graduate who earned two degrees and held a well-paying job as a social worker with the state. It was also true that she held the distinguished position of being the first and only female deacon of her father's renowned and prosperous church, Mount Calvary Baptist of Prince Street.

Unfortunately, she suffered a series of nervous breakdowns following her father's untimely death and from years of physical and emotional abuse by her drug addict husband. The toll of these experiences finally plunged her into despair and she became content to be a destitute folk hero and local bootlegger. Sally also dabbled in tarot card readings and fortune telling, more of a hustle than any serious proclamation for the future. Nonetheless people from the Third Ward who played the daily lottery game would frequently seek her insight in an effort to yield a winning combination for that day's number.

When she entered the Sinclair domain her appearance was disheveled and ragged, a far cry from how she used to look. It was a haunting sight to witness - her holding the baby and smiling; perhaps she smiled because she had no children of her own, or maybe it was refreshing to see a fresh, innocent face that wasn't corrupted by hustling, conning, or selling pussy. The eyes of both parents were cautiously fixed upon her as she held little Charles and they were even more surprised when she blurted out, "He's going to be a lady killer and very successful when he grows up. Those hazel brown eyes and wavy hair will magnetize him to all females."

Over time, her pronouncement proved to be absolutely correct!

Miss Sally gently handed the baby back to Anna with her head bowed as if held in a trance, and then slowly made her exit out the front door.

It wasn't until she had left that Carnell noticed Sally had slid a bottle of homemade gin behind the back cushion of his lounge chair. As soon as he discovered her small token he quickly retrieved two shot glasses and proposed a toast to Anna. This was going to be a special toast to his beautiful lady, free from the male chatter that usually accompanies the toast performed at Dee Dee's Lounge.

"To us," he said, as they lifted and touched their glasses. Anna paused to remove the gin from her glass and replaced it with orange juice.

"Yes," she replied, "all three of us."

As they swallowed their drinks, they turned their attention to Charles, who was asleep upon the soft sofa, worn out from the continued attention he'd received all day. There seemed to be a contented smile upon his caramel-colored face as a result of feeling secure and loved by in the aftermath of events that day.

It was getting late, with sunset approaching and the day winding down. Anna gingerly put the sleeping baby to bed, then decided to get a needed rest for herself.

Carnell shuffled through his jazz collections of 78 RPMs and selected a few of his all-time favorites by Charlie Parker, Miles Davis, and Duke Ellington. He carefully loaded them all onto the General Electric record player, and then cradled himself back into his chair. He reared his head back into the pillows and began to reminisce about his life with Anna as Charlie and Dizzy played on. The up-tempo musical beats playing within that space of peace in their living room moved him to light a Cuban cigar. He casually blew some rings of smoke toward the ceiling as it started coming back to him as to how, where and when they first met.

Their story started after Carnell joined the United States Army at the age of 19 during the month of March in the year of 1942. The devastating attack visited on Pearl Harbor had provoked the ire of the entire nation and many young men were feeling the patriotic duty to join any branch of the United States Armed Services. The mindset of many was to prove their valor and courage and bring about a lasting defeat to Hitler and his Japanese allies.

Among the Negro populace was the idea of fighting for democracy, which in turn would also defeat segregation and bigotry throughout the world, and specifically in the USA. Although at the time the armed forces were strictly segregated, Carnell felt supremely proud to drive supplies to all-white battalions as part of the duties of the red ball express. The red ball express was likened to the red tail air force unit known as the Tuskegee Airmen. The numerous untold stories of their courage and pride to resist defeat and collect victories were essential to ending World War II. Carnell would later be part of the liberation forces for towns in France and Italy.

He was not a big man. He stood at the height of 5'8" tall and weighed a mere 169.

As a solider he was second to none and often fought bravely when called upon. He also was wounded twice and received the Distinguished Service Cross for his bravery. The award was for saving several members of his unit during a machine gunners attack and capture of the enemy's weapons.

The final wounds he received were the result of stepping on an exploding mine. The injury left his left arm partially paralyzed from elbow to fingers.

He left France in 1945 and was scheduled for surgery and rehabilitation at an army hospital located in Havana, Cuba. It was at there that he met Anna and was star struck with the first sight of her.

Anna Diaz was working as a nurse's assistant and moonlighting as a mambo dancer and Afro-Cuban jazz singer at a popular local club. She was stunningly beautiful at 5'1" tall with long, black, silky hair and cocoa-tan skin. She was stacked like a royal racing stallion. Beyond her hourglass figure, shapely legs, and overall gorgeous looks, there was a charming personality accompanied by bi-lingual skills and vivid sense of humor. She and Carnell appeared to be made for each other, and he made it clear from the beginning that he was going to make her his wife and love her eternally.

Miss Diaz proved to be the most effective cure for Carnell's war injuries. After his multiple surgeries she nursed him to health with laughter, listening to his war stories, and displaying some of her dazzling mambo and cha-cha dance moves.

One night while out on the town visiting a local jazz club, Anna stood in for her tardy girlfriend and got the chance to sing a set featuring the legendary Dizzy Gillespie. It was a dream come true appearing with Dizzy's band and to her surprise the audience loved her performance. After that set she was invited to tour Cuba with the band; she turned the offer down because of her commitment to nursing Carnell and her dream of living together with him in the United States.

He referred her to be his "foxy lady" and she tagged him as her "sweet Charlie Brown."

At the conclusion of his six-month rehabilitation, their relationship had grown from admirable intoxication to fully developed romantic love.

In Cuba there weren't any annoying racial critics complaining about this interracial couple and their apparent open love toward one another that was always tastefully on public display. The society was very open and the color spectrum ranged from pale white to dark black; you loved whom you loved and all were at peace supporting that love.

The primary class difference in that society was economic and Anna was from a less wealthy background. She had always had dreams of a different and more comfortable lifestyle. It seemed quite possible that her love with a wounded and decorated World War II veteran might also be the ticket to provide her way out.

All of Anna's immediate family and friends admired Carnell and loved the respect and honor he showed her. They also knew as did Anna that he would provide a better opportunity for her, and everyone anticipated the happy ending that awaited them both.

On several occasions some jealous onlookers who didn't like this foreigner who intruded into their domain would test Carnell's manhood, much to the dismay of Anna's family and friends.

On one such occasion while the couple shopped at a bodega, a drunken local man made an improper gesture toward Anna and placed his hands on her protruding buttocks. Carnell asked the man to apologize but he refused to do so and - to his misfortune - cursed him out in Spanish in front of the other customers.

Little did this man know that Carnell had become very fluent in the Cuban dialect while stationed there, and he knew exactly what was uttered. As Carnell approached this man, two of his buddies decided to come at him and add further harassment. This was an obvious mistake, despite Carnell's wounded arm and small stature.

The fight happened in a flash and with lightning speed. Due to his high-level defensive skills he had learned in the army, he registered a defeat for all three of his larger opponents. He amazingly knocked out one and sent the other two to the emergency room with broken bones.

Anna just stood nearby amazed with her little man, but very proud to know he was her warrior supreme.

News about the incident quickly spread throughout the community and Carnell became a local hero for defeating the three thugs. It wasn't long after the scuffle that he earned the nickname of Big C.

Anna, was feeling like a rescued princess, took her hero home and made passionate love with him throughout the night. As they tossed and tussled in the joys and positions of lovemaking, Carnell paused momentarily and turned toward his foxy lady with the soft brown eyes and said, "This ass belongs to me. And no one will ever touch it but me."

"I am yours," replied his foxy lady, "You can do with this ass whatever you want for as long as you want."

After the healing of his injuries, Big C remained for a little while longer than expected, but before he was ordered to return to the states he surprised Anna with a proposal of marriage.

The moon was in full bloom on this special night in the month of June, and while walking along the beach he stopped, fell upon his knees, and proceeded to pop the question. The glowing full moon and the ocean waves applauding in the background created the perfect backdrop for what he was about to say.

Anna stopped when he fell upon his knees, thinking that something was wrong; when she turned around she noticed his stretched out hands held a sparkling diamond ring. She was so surprised and speechless. She grabbed her mouth in excitement, and then bashfully waited for the magnificent moment.

"I haven't known a lot of women before you," he began. "But I knew deep within my heart that you were meant for me. I'll be strong, tender, protective, and ever loving, if you'll marry me, if you consent to be my ever loving wife."

The shock was too much for Anna and she broke down sobbing. And yet she managed to repeat in Spanish and English, "Si, si, yes, yes, my darling, my sweet Charlie Brown, I will forever be your loving and supportive wife."

He stood up, wrapped his good and bad arm around her and kissed her with all the passion he could muster. There they stood smiling and crying before they fell onto the warm sand below, holding hands and laughing, while gazing up at the winking moon in full glow.

Two months later - on August 29, 1946 - they held a small wedding attended by a few army buddies along with Anna's family and friends from the local club where she worked as a dancer. It was a simple wedding, but the elegance of Anna and Carnell's love for each other made it sublime.

The army chaplain officiated, which made the transition to the states more acceptable and expedited legal matters.

The next stop for the newlyweds would be a major city in New York or somewhere in New Jersey; either would be a good location where Carnell could likely find solid employment and a nice community to live with his beautiful and loving new wife.

After the reminiscing and time travel of Carnell's early beginnings with Anna were waning, he awakened to find her smiling at him with loving eyes. She gestured toward him with swinging hips, holding out her hand and beckoning him to join her in bed. It was as though she had sensed what he was dreaming and wanted her husband to accompany her to that warm, comfortable embrace of her arms. This was the essential way that they connected with one another, each one knowing what the other felt or needed and responding in kind.

Carnell stood up from his favorite chair, stretching his body and then reaching out to embrace his foxy-lady wife. After the embrace they both proceeded to give their son a collective good-night kiss. They looked at one another and said in unison,

"I love you baby, now and forever more."

CHAPTER 3

The early years

During the first years of Charles' growth, his parents doted daily upon their young son. It seemed as if he was their gallant prince and they were his willing entourage.

There was plenty of evidence from this early age that he was developing a unique and structured personality, complete with charm and grace. He was growing into a pleasant, happy, and contented child with a healthy appetite for breast milk and mashed food sautéed with honey and water.

Anna would read her baby all kinds of literature, ranging from daily news briefs, to children's books, and occasionally the Holy Bible. Little Charles would respond with poignant smiles as though he understood every word. He would It point at pictures happily as if agreeing to whatever his mother was reading at the time.

Anna realized the value of the spoken word and her son's response to books. It was also her desire to teach her young son the value of being bi-lingual, as this would broaden both his brain power and social relations. Whenever she would teach him a word in English she would complement it with the same word in Spanish.

He responded with eagerness for learning and expressed fondness of books from a very tender age.

Anna was accustomed to a regular routine of daily house chores with the sounds of jazz and Latin music punctuating the air, filling their home with relaxed rhythms and good vibrations. There was a special fondness for Anna whenever she would sing to her baby bilingually; and that seemed to meet his approval, because, a song was usually followed by a soft, soothing, and comfortable sleep.

Whenever Carnell arrived home from work he would test his son's reactions by tossing him into the air and racing throughout the house with him atop his shoulders as though he was a horse. The boy loved and looked forward to this daily routine of play and it always ended with giggles and laughter.

Both parents agreed that this child would have the balance of spiritual affection combined with physical conditioning, and little Charles would soak it all in every day.

Charles was a mild-mannered young lad and socially well-adjusted among adults or children his age. People would gravitate to him because of his good looks and sense of serenity.

There seemed to be a sense of urgency in young Charles' development. At the age of 9 months, there was a classic demonstration of this kind of precociousness, when he took the first few steps toward his dad. The next few steps were eventful because he stumbled forward and fell down. He was not afraid or intimidated by this mishap and got up immediately to continue walking normally throughout their small Cape Cod home as if he had done it at another time in his life. One could say things happened very easily or naturally for Charles and it wasn't long after those first few steps that he spoke his first English word; and to no one's surprise, it was "Mama."

The early years seemed to vanish quickly, but were frequently and candidly documented by Carnell, who had a passion for cameras and various kinds of recording devices. At any special event or celebration, there would be Carnell with cameras in hand, as if he was Cecil B. De Mille directing a blockbuster Hollywood movie. The most important and precious moments of Charles' young life were captured and preserved within the binders of a scrapbook or on film, in black and white or color. The film library of young Charles chronicled his life from age 1 until just beyond the age of 14.

This film library included many social and family events such as birthday parties, Halloween, Fourth of July, Christmas, summer vacations, and finally his graduation from elementary school. Documenting events became Carnell's hobby and also his way to preserve the family history.

The years would come and go, but he could always turn back the clock through film and still photographs. Whenever there was company over for dinner or drinks, the scrapbook and movie projector would somehow manage to become the focal point of attention, and the attention Charles' photographs received swelled the pride of the Sinclairs.

The phenomenal bonding between Carnell and Charles was a natural transition that began the moment the son arrived from the hospital. It never caused a rift between Anna and Carnell or Anna and Charles; their mutual love and respect for each other would never allow that.

Life had been good to Carnell since his marriage and return to the states.

He bought and furnished a Cape Cod style home through the very effective GI Bill, and was fortunate to work for the United States Post Office as a mail clerk. This kind of work was considered important and secure and was well paid; it provided measurable benefits for a small, middle-income family.

Their home was located in a mixed racial residential neighborhood of professionals and skilled blue-collar workers.

The Sinclair home was easily distinguished by its soft yellow brick color, white shutters and manicured landscaping. It was a corner property with plenty of space surrounding all sides.

The interior design was one of a spacious, open floor plan with a central fireplace. It became the setting for small social gatherings of family and friends, and Carnell and Anna were not shy to host a good party for any occasion.

It was Anna who selected the neighborhood and the home; she always said the coloring was a reminder of her beloved Cuba. Charles had sometimes worked two jobs so that their home would be paid for ahead of schedule and could be inherited by their first born.

The neighborhood was near the edge of town, a mere three blocks away from the infamous Beehive section of the city. These two very different neighborhoods were separated by train tracks. At an earlier time in history the freight trains that carried goods along these tracks signified a major divide of two communities; one White the other Black, one poor and the other privileged.

The small, seedy section of town from which the Beehive evolved was a red-light district without the red lights. It was inhabited by various kinds of criminals, big and small, who all managed, employed, and profited from a full range of illegal activities.

Underscoring the paradox of these two different neighborhoods was Dee Dee's Lounge, located in the heart of the area. This was where Big C spent some of his favorite times, enjoying a cold brew and small talk with the fellas. The dilemma that would haunt him in the near future would be keeping his associations at Dee Dee's and guarding his son from the influence of gangsters. This endeavor would become a juggling act quite different than any Carnell had experienced in the military, but he would remain vigilant in his efforts to shield his son from harm.

Throughout his youth more often than he desired, Charles would hear the words of wisdom from his father's mouth: "Be smart, stay alert, and avoid the Beehive. This is not for you and I expect you to do better.

"Remember; your education is the key to unlocking your dreams."

As Charles began the early years of adolescence his father was very proud and comfortable having him along as willing company. Each year, young Charles was looking and acting more like his father. As a result of their natural bonding, he was beginning to imitate many of Carnell's social manners and personality traits.

Saturdays were generally reserved for their dates at the neighborhood barbershop; on other occasions they'd shop and purchase matching outfits. They also enjoyed various sporting events, especially baseball; and of course a matinee showing of a good western or horror movie.

At 15 years of age Charles was walking, smiling, and using body and hand gestures in the same mode as his father. When people saw them the response was usually, "My, how you have grown" or "you look so much like your father," or the all-time favorite, "I saw you both from the rear and I couldn't tell who was who."

It was only natural that these compliments engaged Carnell's pride and prompted him to stick out his chest an inch or two more. He would just say, "thank you," and his smiling would give hints as to how he really felt. As the two stood side by side, Charles was only an inch and a half shorter, but was developing muscles and body weight in all the right places.

A few years earlier a younger Charles had been busy shining shoes on Saturdays at the barbershop or operating the lemonade stand in front of the house. He didn't mind learning how to earn an honest dollar or two, a responsible life value his father had nurtured in him. Yes, he was growing up and becoming a responsible adolescent heading toward the teenage years with all of their complexities.

In elementary school, Charles was a fine student, receiving excellent grades. He was admired by both his teachers and peers. The subject that he excelled in was math and he also had a strong aptitude for history. In his spare time he developed a knack for art and design, and would dabble in water-color paints and charcoal sketches of anything that caught his eye.

It was in the third grade that Charles met his best friend for life, O'Neil. He was a small framed, shy, and skinny Asian-American kid, who was a bit taller than Charles. The two of them were inseparable, spending time earning money doing odd jobs for neighbors, enjoying sleepovers, riding their bicycles throughout the communities and often studying their favorite subject of math together.

The neighbors would often tease them about their bonding times together, saying they were beginning to act and look alike. O'Neil was like a brother to Charles and vice-versa; he was nicknamed Lid by Charles because of how he wore his hat and caps tightly covering his head and eyes. Neither had any brothers or sisters or a large family base, which was an important thread in their bonding.

Their close friendship was fostered by the fact they lived only three doors away from each other and spent an equal amount of time at one another's home. It was O'Neil who also gave Charles his nickname; he called him Chop saying he was so small he looked as if he was chopped from something bigger. By the time they entered high school and Charles had grown a little taller, their friends and associates had changed that name to CJ, the initials of his first and middle names.

Promotion from elementary to high school was filled with complexities for both CJ and O'Neil. In elementary school life was free and easy going, but now the attraction or distractions of pretty girls, sports and the natural hormonal changes seemed to dominate their daily lives. The greatest challenge for CJ and O'Neil at high school was focus.

Each day was anything but routine at Crispus Attucks High School, one of the largest schools in the city. It had a mixed population of high, middle, and low income and was racially mixed as well. In spite of their diversity, most of the students and staff seemed to get along.

Neither of the two best friends were athletes at Attucks High, but they did play basketball for their community centers and the Third Ward Boys Clubs.

At school CJ was a dominant player for the chess team; he always enjoyed the kinds of mental exercises and challenges that were rewarded with bragging rights at the conclusion of a competitive match. He also engaged himself in becoming a photographer for the high school newspaper and yearbook committee. With plenty of social and physical activities provided at school, boredom would seem hard to come by.

CJ was as popular at CAHS as he was at the elementary school. He was maturing into a very handsome, secure, and self-confident young man with established goals in mind for the future. He had learned from his father the values of coordinated clothing, color matching, and how to be well groomed. And as a result, at the end of each school year at Attucks High, CJ was named the best dressed of his class.

During those years, other types of eyes were being focused on CJ; and, unfortunately, he never had a clue.

There was a storm brewing and heading straight for CJ, and it would prove to be more demanding and paradoxical than any chess match could ever be.

What was this? It was the natural and divine balance created and structured for humankind; one that can bring peace and serenity or chaos beyond reprieve. It is the natural and opposite attraction; it is the female in all their splendor, glory, and power.

It is a proven biological fact that males and females mature quite differently, and at paces that are completely non-parallel. It is also true and quite evident that females are measurably out in front of the males. This applies to the emotions, thought processes, and physical hormonal development.

As an Eastern philosopher ounce said, "Females are the prime initiators. They can be alpha and omega, long before we recognize anything."

One of the primary goals of human development is to harness energy and forge relationships with other human beings. Our innate five senses grow and expand into unknown regions of the brain when the opposite sex enters the equation.

The beauty, smell, taste, and touch excites and heightens our senses to such a stimulated point that we become unfamiliar with logic, rationality, or even at times just plain common sense.

'All of these biological and emotional changes lead to one result: adolescent love. A unique and new experience, at a new time in Charles' yet young and ever-changing life was about to unfold while presenting a new realization of himself and the world around him.

A beautiful, talented, and smart young female would become the recipe for this change in the way that a caterpillar changes into the beautiful soaring, fluttering, butterfly - a change that no one could foresee.

CHAPTER 4

First love

Becoming aware of CJ and his newly discovered female companion would surprise everyone, especially Anna and Carnell.

Although there was a genuine sparkle to CJ's personality, mannerisms, and sense of cool, he was a relatively quiet, shy-natured individual. He generally seemed to be preoccupied with the likes of chess matches, math equations, and photography.

it was totally unexpected that a female interest would ever occur at this time. It wasn't that girls were not attracted to him; after all he was a good looking, fashionable dresser who spoke two languages and possessed a unique high IQ. He was friendly, polite, and often charming without being pretentious or egotistical - the type of young man that anyone would be proud to introduce to their parents.

It was ironic, however, that this particular young lady would be the one to cast her net forward and reel him in. She was a transfer student who had recently arrived from a neighboring state and rival high school.

She had first noticed Charles two years earlier, when he was intensely focused on competing for a first-place trophy at the annual regional chess tournament. The attraction she felt for CJ was real and immediate, and she jumped at the opportunity to introduce herself to him so that she could examine him with a much closer look.

"Hi. My name is Cynthia DeHaviland," she said as she extended her hand.

"Congratulations on your first-place trophy. You are a really good chess player, and I've always had a desire to learn some day. Do you give lessons, and where do you practice?"

She was looking at him from head to toe, with all the admiration she could muster; her white teeth glowed and she smiled the smile of a cat who was about to eat the canary. If the first impressions are the ones to last, then she wanted this one to be eternal!

"Excuse me," replied CJ.

Astonished by her direct approach, he shook her hand and attempted to answer her questions.

"My name is Charles Jesus Sinclair; but my friends call me CJ.

"Thank you very much, but I'm not from around here; I live in New Jersey."

"Well that's not too far from here, and I have relatives I often visit in New Jersey," Cynthia said. "Since I know what school you're from, perhaps we'll see one another someday soon."

"OK," replied CJ.

She was stunningly beautiful and he could barely take his eyes off of her, but he briefly looked away because he didn't want to be rude. As his sight returned squarely on her, he found himself smiling at her in an unusual way. She was still holding his hand, which had now become warm all over. He slowly began removing his hand as he felt the softness of hers leaving a pleasant void.

"Unfortunately, my bus is waiting for me and I have to leave," he said. "It was nice meeting you."

"Oh sure, and it was my pleasure meeting you, too."

As CJ quickened his steps toward the bus he turned around to take a last look, he was surprised to notice Cynthia's eyes locked onto him; she was smiling, glowing, and waving furiously.

Once he boarded the bus and was being congratulated by his coaches and teammates he forgot about his pleasant interlude.

Two years later, Charles was beginning his senior year in high school, a year more important than the previous three years for a multitude of reasons. It was a year akin to a rite of passage as he began his journey into adulthood and responsibility while shedding the skin of immaturity and adolescence. Like most students, he faced significant choices concerning college, military service, marriage, and employment.

One early fall school day as CJ was exiting his guidance counselor's office after contemplating his decision whether to attend college or not, he accidently bumped into a student, knocking her books to the floor.

He scrambled to retrieve the mess he caused and was apologizing in the process, when the girl looked up and noticed who it was.

"I'm sorry," said CJ; "I wasn't looking where I was going."

He didn't recognize who he was talking with, and continued to pick up papers and books. As they both lifted their heads and came face to face, she cried out, "CJ, is that you?"

She would have recognized him in a crowd of 2,000 people.

Cynthia had never forgotten their first encounter and was anticipating seeing him again ever since that championship chess tournament of two years earlier. She had made a solemn vow to see him again and was determined and confident it would happen no matter the situation or circumstances.

Finally, her dream day had arrived and she was convinced to seize this opportunity and to fully embrace it.

CJ, however, was surprised and overwhelmed that she knew his name, as he hadn't yet recognized who this person was.

"It's me, Cynthia. Don't you recognize me?"

In that moment CJ was completely embarrassed, and still unsure of this beautiful female that stood before him. The scent of her perfume was intoxicating; she was well dressed with small amounts of makeup applied perfectly upon her smiling face.

The moment she extended her hand and they touched, it ignited sensuous warmth that quickly refreshed his sense of memory. He couldn't recall if she was this beautiful two years ago; and it didn't matter because she was now, and he was grateful that he had caused such a mess.

Cynthia had matured, more voluptuous than he remembered, and her hair style was different. She was not wearing glasses this time and she appeared to be taller, but still shorter than CJ. She had a caramel color skin with beautiful black, long, curly hair. Her smile would light up the night sky.

To put it bluntly, CJ was mesmerized and unusually nervous.

"Oh yes," he blurted out. "Now I do; at first I didn't recognize you.

"What on earth are you doing here at Carver High?" How have you been? And, oh yes, I apologize for the accident. Wow! You are so beautiful," he bashfully proclaimed, while continuing to feel the warmth of her soft little hands.

It was what she had waited so long to hear, and the sound of his voice, the sparkle in his light brown eyes, made her tingle all over.

All of this took place in a matter of a few seconds, but it seemed as though time had stood still.

After an extended sigh of relief and a long slow exhale, she reluctantly released his hand from hers. Maintaining eye contact, she replied, "I was looking down at my class schedule and I didn't see you. I believe I have lunch next period."

"That's fantastic," said CJ. "It is also my lunch period. Can I join you?"

"Of course, you can; if you don't join me I will be offended."

"Well, I wouldn't want to do that"

CJ held out his hand once again for her and she responded warmly and invitingly, as the two of them walked slowly toward the school cafeteria for lunch and plenty of conversation.

When they entered the cafeteria, it felt as though all eyes were suddenly upon them. It didn't matter to them that some eyes were curious or that some were envious; they were in their own world.

The two of them talked for the duration of their 40-minute lunch period, sipping on soda and smiling a lot.

In the course of their developing conversations there was much to exchange and share about their lives and families. CJ learned that Cynthia was a daughter of military parents who were being moved and transferred around the country and even around the world. She had lived in six different cities and changed schools four times since her days as an elementary school student.

There was, she said, the issue of her aging grandmother who was wrestling with an illness, so her parents thought it a good idea if she spent her senior year by her side. It was sheer coincidence that Cynthia's residence was now in New Jersey in a city near Carver High School. She had arranged to transfer to Carver High with the anticipation of eventually seeing and spending time with CJ.

Cynthia believed that their re-acquaintance was due to fate and predestination while Charles simply thought it was his good fortune. In the up-coming months they would spend as much quality time together as possible, enjoying their common interests and new discoveries.

The news of CJ and his new girlfriend traveled around the town like a bullet; and before he could properly make the introductions to mom and dad, it was too late. One evening when he arrived from chess practice, Anna and Big C met him at the front doorway with peering eyes and grins on their faces.

"How's my darling son doing these days?" said Anna, and then Carnell chimed in,

"What's up son? Is there anything new going on in your life?"

CJ knew immediately that something was brewing. He quickly figured it out and they all laughed out loud together.

Anna was the first to investigate and she jumped right in.

"I heard about your new friend, Cynthia; When can we get the opportunity to meet her?" she asked.

"Where is she from, how old is she, and is she good looking?" added Carnell.

Charles began laughing again as he reached out to hug his two most beloved people in the world.

"Don't worry guys, she can't replace you, and I will always love you more."

"I would like to invite her for dinner, along with her grandmother. Is that alright with you two?"

"Sure!" they replied in unison. "How about next weekend? Let's plan on Saturday at 6 o'clock; OK?"

"All right; I'll inform her, and it's officially a date."

CJ paused for a moment then said, "I'll have to see if her grandmother can make it; her illness has her down a lot."

"Well, if she can't that's all right; I'm sure we'll have plenty to focus on with Miss Cynthia," Anna said with a smile.

The dinner was a big hit for the Sinclair family; it was the first time CJ invited anyone for dinner other than his friend O'Neil.

Anna got to thoroughly examine the young lady who was tugging on her son's heart strings. As expected, Carnell was easier on Cynthia. (Fathers usually are in matters like these.) He simply adored her and thought she would make a good addition to the Sinclair clan. The mature, lady-like charm and grace of Cynthia had relaxed Anna and Carnell throughout the evening of film sessions about CJ's life and topics of personnel interest concerning her family history.

The family of four got off to a good start and as Cynthia was leaving Anna let out a sigh of relieve and shed a few tears. She was holding Carnell around his waist with her head resting against his shoulder as they waved goodnight. After taking a deep breath she softly said to Big C, "Look at our baby, honey; he's growing up to be a fine young man."

"Yeah, baby, he is."

At that moment Carnell reared his head back with laughter and said, "And it looks like he has a fine young lady right next to him."

Anna just smiled because she felt something positive from Cynthia as well and any anxieties that she may have had before meeting her began to ease.

The dinner date and meeting CJ's girlfriend had affected Big C differently than it did Anna. It enabled him to see his son through a different lens and appreciate that he and Anna had done a good job of raising him. A couple of weeks later he invited CJ to accompany him down to Dee Dee's Lounge for a toast with the fellas.

Carnell had never shared a drink with CJ before, but he was now thinking that his age of 19 and relative maturity would make that acceptable. Despite the fact that the legal drinking age in the state of New Jersey was still 21, it didn't concern Big C that anyone at Dee Dee's would mind.

He was feeling more relaxed about the influences of shady and criminal characters from the Beehive section of town. He thought to himself that with CJ dating and preparing for graduation and possible college selection he would be too preoccupied to even care or notice.

The main issue for Big C was his desire to expand their bonding and fellowship - now that his son was becoming a respectable, responsible young man.

This was a sweet time for the Sinclair family; things were changing and the future was looking good. It was the perfect opportunity for reflecting, toasting, celebrating, and looking forward. The overall effect of these changes in their collective lives felt like sampling a fresh jar of honey made by the bees' hard work; and once you taste it you gladly and simply proclaim: "How sweet it is."

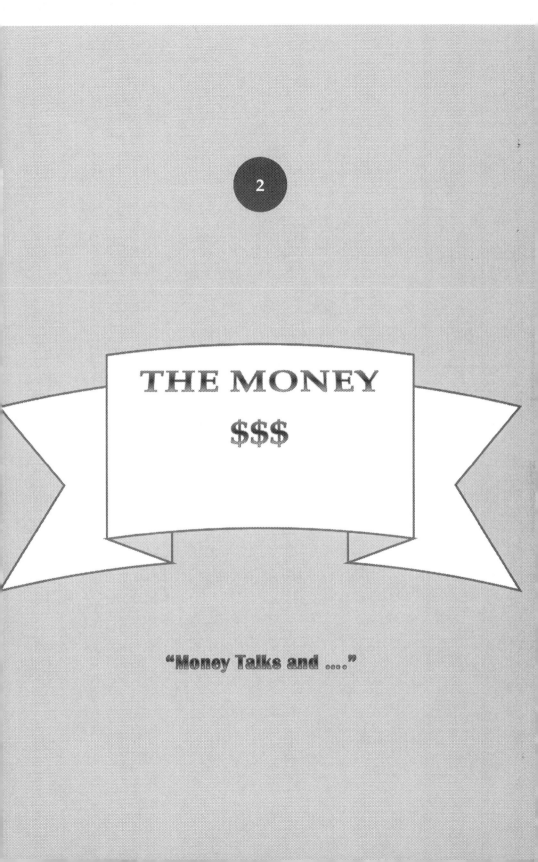

2

THE MONEY
$$$

"Money Talks and ...."

CHAPTER 5

The introduction

The euphoric atmosphere at the Beehive typically begins to swell and come alive on Friday evenings, although there is plenty of sin and vice taking place throughout the week. The start of most weekends requires a different mindset than other days of the week, simply because the eagle flies on Fridays and many people have acquired enough money to freely spend.

This area of the city sparkles with a carnival-like energy. It is here that all of the movers, shakers, and suckers swagger deep into the night, ready to take and be taken.

The suggestion that Carnell made to CJ for a toast at Dee Dee's was for him to witness this display with his father by his side to protect and ward off any type of prowlers. It was also his idea to alert everyone that this was his son - and that he would not be set up as an easy mark.

This was Charles' first time ever venturing into this part of the city and it was expected that he would possibly be awed and excited. CJ was very smart and inquisitive, and after scanning the street with his eyes and turning his head to see all he could, he simply asked what he thought was an intelligent question; "Why this area is named the Beehive?"

This question seemed to puzzle Carnell momentarily, causing him to stop walking as he retraced his memory of the legend he had heard many times in the past.

"No one can recall how the name Beehive was applied to this section of town or how long it has been in effect," he began. "The elders of the community seem to recall it was coined by a police officer who noted that the types of characters and their activities were reminiscent of bees swarming around their hives right before they began making honey.

"Over the many years this name has stuck and the popularity has grown to accompany its overall corruption."

As the sun begins to drop below the horizon and reflects a soft, dusky glow in the night sky, its departure marks the beginning of a countdown to a colorful spectacle of glamor, glitz, and gloom, which would last until the following sunrise.

An array of sordid rank and file of these willing participants ascends each night onto the concrete walks and black asphalt streets, staking out territories, pitted against rivals and anticipating new arrivals.

The nightly routine rarely becomes dull or boring as they stroll toward the 'Hive singly, doubled, or in small packs. The area of this scene is relatively small, consisting of a mere three blocks on a wide street appropriately dubbed Broadway.

There is an oddity in the names and types of businesses on display, which forms a camouflage to the kinds of activities that actually take place. Along the Broadway strip are stores that bear such names as The Sugar Cane, Cut and Curl, The Pony Express, and the infamous Heads Up. The establishments provide an outlet for gambling, drinking, jazz music, and various forms of vice and prostitution. The mixture and variation of the patrons who assemble at these places is the true representation of an integrated society that reflects who we are and how we like to be entertained.

The people are a wide mix of racial, business, and cultural backgrounds. On any given night - and especially on weekends - CEOs and other high-ranking officers from the corporate and business domains come to Broadway. Many local and state elected officials who control government appear and participate weekly as honored guests.

Last are the social non-elites - the blue collar employees and everyday working class people, who are the most loyal and largest group. There is no discrimination at any of the establishments; only your money is the passport to social delights for the evening.

Businesses in the Beehive look like regular retail stores when patrons enter; but, once inside, a secret, paneled, sound-proofed wall or door opens and allows the patrons to walk into a completely different and controlled environment. The interior designs incorporate above-standard-quality materials - the best that money can buy.

The decor is unique in each. The Sugar Cane is loaded with imported Italian inlaid flooring, well-lit designer chandeliers, oak wood tables, colorful stages for live music, and a dance floor that can support at least 75 customers. All of the competing locations are fashionably designed in the finest taste; all aim to please their specific types of clientele.

The high and low rollers who frequent these places come from as far away as Chicago and as near as New York. The primary reason to visit the Beehive is for social esteem, bragging rights, and for having the time of your life by doing things that you normally would not or could not do.

Outside of the occasional raid by greedy police from neighboring districts, the Beehive seldom disappointed any of its patrons.

Carnell parked his car several blocks away and he and CJ strolled along Broadway, while he pointed out the highlights of the Beehive.

"Do you see that building with all the candy in the window? said Carnell.

"Yes," replied CJ.

"Well, that's The Sugar Cane, and it's the busiest nightclub in the Beehive. The owners named it The Sugar Cane, not because of the candy, but because of the gambling, drinking, and jazz music that takes place inside. The candy store is a front; but right behind the store and well hidden from public view are various types of illegal slot machines, roulette wheels, poker games, and the sweetest live jazz music outside of New York City."

As they continued the tour along Broadway, CJ noticed the fancy-colored Cadillacs that slowly moved along, allowing onlookers to sneak a peek and offer an occasional wave. There was one particular vehicle that captured his attention immediately. It was a custom-made, off-white colored Jaguar fully equipped with chrome accents splashed about the exterior, a telephone inside, and bullet-proof glass all around.

The rear window was lowered slightly - enough to display the leopard design and beige leather interior. This luxury car was moving slower than the others and was chauffer driven. Sitting comfortably, relaxed in the rear, was a tall, tan, and well-dressed Negro male who was blowing smoke rings from a fat cigar while admiring the nightly scenes along the Broadway.

CJ was intrigued, and so he asked, "Hey, Dad, who is that man?"

"That my son is today's number one manager of all that you see here. He owns many of these buildings and they call him Bootsy, because he likes to wear tailor made, imported boots from Europe. There are rumors that the tips of his boots are made with a special metal that is sharpened to a razors edge - and that he has used them more than once to kill or injure people.

"He is also very protected by the police and judges, and some say he was once a collection-man for the mob," Carnell continued. "He is the kingpin of the pimps and hustlers who control and manipulate the Beehive.

"Bootsy has become filthy rich because he receives nearly 20 percent of all profits made here, and he is an ally of the New York Italian mobsters."

"Wow!" was the only response that CJ could utter, however there was a gleam of excitement in his brown eyes as he continued looking on. His father had noticed this response from his son and realized that he could be vulnerable and possibly influenced by what he was seeing.

"This is not for you, CJ. I'm showing you all this so you will avoid it. I would hope you will do something more constructive with your life."

"I will, Dad, don't worry. I will."

The minutes passed into the night; the Beehive was swarming with life as Big C and his impressionable son continued their stroll down the infamous Broadway. There was a distinct air of arrogance and untouchability hoovering above the heads of those who were mingling about and going to and fro.

The long, shiny, elegant Cadillac and Lincoln Continental cars were now increasing in numbers and styles as they paraded along Broadway; and some were casually parked in front of the main businesses that Carnell would be pointing out. Occasionally, the drivers and the passengers would exit their cars and stand nearby. The purpose for this was to show possession and to display their latest fashionable wardrobes under the bright street lights. This had become a guaranteed nightly, free fashion show.

The high-end fashions worn by the men and women was a routine feature, and spectators would show up regularly to take full notice. It was obvious to the on-lookers that these clothes weren't bought from the local haberdashers, but rather from custom designers worldwide. The color schemes were usually of the brightest spectrums: lime greens, hot pinks. Soft yellows and sky blues were accented by pinstripe or sharkskin fabrics.

The shoes were made by of alligator, snake, or elephant skin. The men normally would wear a stingily brimmed hat designed by Du'Capa or wide brimmed styles by Kangol. The walking stick was the complementary feature to these wardrobes; and it was a topped by white pearl, gold, or a diamond-studded handle. The accessories of rings, watches, or other jewelry were always of the large variety and sparkled throughout the night.

The women, not to be outdone, would often compete against the men in fashion color palettes, hair styles, jewelry, and shoes. The fur stoles, hats, and dresses on display were the top of the line - and always imported from Paris or Italy. These women who came out for a night of frolic and pleasure were not prostitutes or street walkers; they were professional and business women of means and status.

The location that received the most notice was Cut and Curl, an upscale and profitable brothel disguised as a co-ed hair and beauty salon. From the street entrance, it appeared to be a pleasant looking, normal beauty salon with regular customers sitting in chairs awaiting their scheduled appointments day or night. This establishment also had a secret access through the bathrooms that led prospective customers to the three floors above. Upon arrival at a selected floor, green or red lights directed them to waiting prostitutes.

The coded name used for this house of vice and by its political connected, high-paying customers was The United Nations, because of the range of ethnic representation by the whores who worked there. The madam was Ms. Betty McQueen, who preferred to be addressed as Madame Butterfly. The ladies who worked for her were loyal and received good care; they never worked the streets with pimps, who could become abusive and violent.

CJ was becoming more inquisitive and excited with each step along Broadway; and he wondered to himself how his dad knew all of this. Finally he asked the obvious question: "Hey, Dad, how do you know all this? Have you ever been to these places?"

"No son, I haven't been to any of them. But the guys who frequent Dee Dee's tell me all of their stories. And I believe them."

CJ thought for a moment, and then followed with another puzzling question: "If all of this is illegal, then how is it possible that the police don't shut it down?"

"The main reason it operates with impunity is because these places make tens of thousands of dollars each week; and the graft and corruption keep them going.

"The police are on the weekly payroll and they receive more money than their regular jobs pay them. "The other reason is because the local politicians often frequent these places - and they like the services that are offered."

That wasn't the answer that CJ was expecting, but he accepted it for the moment as his head continued to turn in every direction, trying not to miss anything.

The tour through the Beehive district was almost coming to an end, but Carnell wanted to show CJ two more major components. The last two business of interest were located in the final block of the district.

One of the oldest centers of illegal activities in major cities throughout the USA is the lottery scam, also known as the numbers game. The numbers game is believed to have originated in the state of Louisiana a decade before the 1920s. Over the years it had grown to become a widespread gambling institution in predominately Negro neighborhoods. The profits generated from this daily scheme are netted in millions of dollars, which makes it a targeted enterprise for organized white gangsters.

Playing the numbers is a daily ritual among people of every race and economic status.

Placing a small bet on a number or series of numbers was the habit of choice for Carnell and Anna each and every day. There were times when they were lucky enough to win and receive a tenfold profit on their nominal bet.

The daily number was the common point of daily inquiry in the neighborhood. A typical conversation would sound like this:

"Hey, man, what was the number last night?"

"It was 287"

"Oh shit, I played 288."

"The other night, I hit for a quarter and won for $250. It was just in time to pay my rent!"

There would be similar conversations all over town. Players didn't hit or collect winnings every day, but they sure would sound that way.

The numbers game has often been referred to as the poor man's racetrack. The irony of that is the winning numbers for any given day had to correspond to the attendance gate that day at the horse track. The gate attendance number was always posted in the sport section of every daily newspaper.

Everyone in town knew, the place to bet your numbers was The Pony Express.

The building that housed The Pony Express was once a bank, and it was well equipped with vaults and strong steel safes. The interior space was designed for off-track race betting with TV monitors for horses that would run throughout the Tri-State area. There were also rooms for featured greyhound racing in Florida and Connecticut. A variety of races took place daily and the bets would range from $2.00 per race to upwards of $2,000.

The numbers game had different operators who roamed their territories with slips of paper to record a person's betting numbers for that day. As the day was ending and the tracks were closing, the number man would return to the bank and deposit all the slips, coins, and dollar bills used for placing bets.

The title of numbers man held different meanings. Some people viewed him to be a common, everyday criminal. Others looked upon him as somewhat of an insurance provider - one who would be available if and when you ever needed his help.

He was a community hero; and if your rent was overdue because you got laid off you called the numbers man. If your man got arrested for gambling or drunkenness and you needed bail money, you called the numbers man.

The numbers man was easy to spot, wearing tailored suits and driving a big, fine Cadillac. The business of being a numbers man, or runner, was extremely lucrative and the policy banks reeled in millions of tax free money each year.

The last of the primary businesses in the Beehive for was a stripper's lounge and pornographic extravaganza affectionately known as Heads up. The uniqueness of this lounge is that it was open to homosexual and heterosexual activities that ran the full spectrum of consensual sexual behaviors. The Heads up lounge was frequented by women more than men. It was known for filming the most bizarre acts of sexual engagements, whether done publicly or privately.

The open sexual activities taking place inside this lounge involved topless and bottomless pole dancing, arranged threesome or couples intercourse with males or females, and viewing booths for watching pornographic films of previous customers. The atmosphere was completely reckless and drugs of all varieties could be purchased and consumed openly. Strip poker was played in full view, and oral and anal sex videos played on wide screens throughout the lounge.

The money made from the assorted vices and crimes couldn't be underestimated or accounted for; it was generally assumed to be in the millions. There always seemed to be plenty of hush money available to keep police and prosecutors at bay, no matter how many raids were done or citations served. It was a sexual vice paradise of wide proportions and the profit margins would insure its continuance.

Bouncers - many of them former professional security men, professional wrestlers, and varied marital artists of the highest degrees - would not hesitate for a moment to send a customer to the emergency room for disruptive behavior. It was also a rare occasion when high-ranking officials or other prominent people frequented Heads Up, but if any had a notion to do so they could reserve VIP rooms at an adjoining private property and indulge in their most pleasurable fantasies.

In the vicinity of Heads Up, CJ and Carnell witnessed the provocative behavior of open prostitution. As a 19-year-old, CJ was naïve about all that his father was pointing out and couldn't believe what he was seeing. He was troubled watching the aggressive, prowling hookers along Broadway while they attracted their prospective johns. After all, Anna was a role model mother who embodied sophistication and style, and he had always respected women in general, holding them in the highest regard.

These ladies of the night were dressed in their scandalous outfits and overdone makeup, and it was all designed to serve the lustful desires of any who wanted to buy. Long legs, short skirts, bared bosoms, fishnet stockings, and wild and colorful wigs were designed to excite at will the men and women who pursued the hookers on Broadway.

Standing nearby and observing very carefully were the pimps who owned them and for whom they so desperately toiled. The prostitutes' only aim of every night was to please their pimps by depositing all nightly earnings into their pockets. Theoretically, these hustlers and pimps would in return stand by for protection and promotion of their ladies' trade, in case something went terribly wrong.

The truth is that on many occasions it was the ladies who needed protection from a vengeful and angry pimp who would publicly berate and cut and bruise any whore of his choosing. The mind games that were played on these women would usually work toward the pimp's interest, as he continued to destroy the self-esteem or innocence of these young women. It was a continuous cycle of abuse and exploitation that had been going on for decades with no end in sight.

The competition between rivals was fierce and sometimes bloody, as the girls would fight over the Johns, waving and beckoning them into their cars; any and all types of available spaces would serve the need for the performed acts of desire.

Fighting also raged over any pimp the women desired to serve; it was what they referred to as being his bottom bitch or highest money-earning whore.

There was no discrimination of color or ethnicity to these working slaves; they represented White, Black, and Hispanic and Asian heritages. They worked hard for their money and the choice was simply a matter of price and time.

Carnell was careful at explaining to CJ one major flaw in this dangerous labor force arrangement: "If a Negro pimp had White women working for him, then that was considered as white slavery. And if he was caught, would serve more time in jail or be exiled to another state."

"Well that's not fair," replied CJ. "And anyway, what difference does color make?"

That's a discussion for another time son; but color always makes a difference."

Big C continued the tour, explaining that the ladies often found that the use of alleyways and cars would solve the space problem for a quick fix; and if not, then there was a nearby motel or hotel for an extended period of time and for more money.

There is obviously no way of exacting what a pimp's weekly or yearly income could be; however, from the looks of their clothing, houses, and big fancy cars, the guess is that there was plenty - and all of it was tax free.

The guided tour was nearly complete and there were many questions that CJ still wanted to ask his knowledgeable father. But he chose not to do so; and he just let out a long breath and tried to absorb what he had witnessed during the tour of the infamous Beehive.

"Hey son, there is the sign of Dee Dee's Lounge straight ahead. I almost forgot where we were headed."

"I think I could use that toast, Dad. It's been a night to remember."

"I hope so son, I thought it best if you learned it from me first. And, of course, I hope you never have a desire to visit there."

From this experience, there were two things that CJ would hold dear to his heart; the first was the quality of time spent with his father, and the other was the knowledge of what goes on in that section of his hometown. That evening CJ had grown wiser and more alert to things that he was once naïve or ignorant about and felt grateful for what was generally taken for granted - namely the love and guidance from his mother and father. CJ would bid adieu to the glamour and vice of the Beehive, but in the not too distant future he would become involved with many of its enterprises, and with his vision and intelligence, he would elevate the Beehive business district to a new level of success.

As the evening began to wane and father and son headed toward Dee Dee's Lounge, CJ had resolved to submit to the wishes of his father and make a toast to the beginning of his new-found love and his emerging manhood.

Carnell put his arms around the shoulders of his son and the two of them walked in the direction of that special place of Carnell's that place where all sorrows melted and a sense of fellowship and joy could reign. That was Dee Dee's Lounge.

CHAPTER 6

Sal the pal

Because the environment of Dee Dee's was pleasant and comfortable, the lounge became a sanctuary away from the crowds and the questionable businesses in the Beehive. It was a home away from home, where life was never complicated. Even the movers and shakers from the other clubs and businesses would convene at Dee Dee's for relaxation, a cold brew, and shared stories about the victories or defeats of their day.

Carnell hadn't been there in a couple of weeks, due to the overtime that he was working at the post office. The money he earned was for a surprise gift he planned for his loving wife. He had promised her years ago that one day they would return to Cuba and celebrate their anniversary.

As he and CJ walked through the doors, he immediately noticed the interior makeover his favorite place had undergone. The bar had a new curved shape and new stools. The floor was shining anew as a result of replacing the old linoleum with vinyl parquet. New lighting made the inside look much bigger and brighter, and larger round tables accented with new tablecloths and small lanterns helped create a welcoming feel of calmness and fun.

Interior changes were a result of a windfall from the lucky number of 287 that Artie and Dee Dee hit, collecting a grand total of $5,000.

It was during the month of April on a Friday night in the year 1974, and some people at the lounge were rejoicing in that feeling of relief from a harsh and cold winter. Others were there celebrating an early income tax refund that had put extra money into their pockets. Whatever the reason for the crowd at Dee Dee's, it was larger than normal and twice as lively.

Carnell and Charles were met with a thunderous greeting from everyone as the two strolled into the newly decorated Dee Dee's Lounge.

"Hey, Big C!"

"What's happening, my man?"

Carnell smiled at everyone, tipped his hat to the crowd and navigated his way to the bar for a place for two. CJ was somewhat surprised by the response, but felt good to know that his dad was welcomed and popular. It was his first time ever being inside of a bar and the look of shyness was evident as he began looking over the patrons who were occupied with drinking, talking, and having a good time. The sounds of jazz were melodiously playing from a new sound system that had finally replaced the old juke box. Many couples were dancing and simply enjoying the freedom that flowed with mellowing sounds that filled the air.

Artie and Dee Dee tended the bar, working feverishly to comply with orders being placed by their customers. They both greeted Big C with a nod and a smile and then Artie asked, "Who is this young blood?"

"This is my one and only 19-year old son, CJ."

"Well, well! Is this little Charles?" asked Dee Dee, greeting him with her pearly white smile and complimentary charm. "Well he is too good looking to be yours; maybe he belongs to Anna!"

They all laughed together while embarrassing CJ in the same moment.

"Where the hell have you been?"

"Don't you love us anymore?"

"You know that I love you. But I love that extra money even more!"

"I'll say an Amen to that," responded Artie, as they all laughed aloud once again.

"I came down to offer a toast to my son for doing so well at school and finding a new love in his life, other than Anna and myself.

"Oh shit," said Dee Dee. "Be careful son; women can be tricky. And they can be twice as complicated."

"Don't tell the young man that" said Artie. "Just be patient and enjoy her as much as you can. After all, nothing in life last forever."

One moment Charles looked a bit confused by what he was hearing concerning women, trying to digest what Dee Dee was saying, and the next moment he was nodding his head in approval as though he understood. It was the thought of his new- found love Cynthia and what he was feeling for her in that brief moment that made him smile.

"I think he got the message," said Dee Dee.

"But only time will tell," Artie responded.

The four of them shared some heartfelt laughter.

Eventually the regular customers at Dee Dee's spotted Carnell at the bar and one by one came over to greet him and CJ.

Carnell was pleased to see everyone, but he particularly wanted to introduce CJ to a few special people.

There was one customer who was drawing more attention than others and he seemed to be enjoying every minute. Despite the noise and clamor of this Friday night crowd, a tall heavily built, dark Black man had recognized Carnell and began walking to where he was sitting. His style and manner, his attire and his confident demeanor made him look important. He didn't have to struggle getting to the bar because people paved a path for him, making his access to Big C easy.

"My man!" he shouted, and then opened his arms to receive and give a big hug. The two men hugged and embraced each other as Carnell seemed to disappear within the frame of this big man. After a few moments of small talk, Carnell invited him to join them at the bar.

"Please allow me to introduce you to my son, Charles Jesus Sinclair We call him CJ."

"Hello young man, my name is Mike Morrison. And they call me Easy Money."

Carnell explained to CJ that he had just met the number one number banker in the city. Most people who had a desire to play the numbers would look forward to playing with Easy Money. There were many past occasions when Mike helped out the family if there was a financial crisis or need of extra money. The common thread between Mike and Anna was that they both had family ties to Cuba. It had been a while since he and Carnell shared a drink and a good conversation, and Mike hadn't seen CJ since he was a small boy.

"How have you been? Is the family alright? Do you need anything?"

"No thank you," replied Carnell.

"We're here tonight to have a father and son toast amongst friends."

Mike and Carnell had become good friends over the years. They began talking of CJ's success as a student and his continuing success as a chess champion.

"Well, what are we waiting for; let's get this party started."

At this time, Easy Money asked Artie to lower the music so he could get everyone's attention.

"May I have everyone's attention please?"

As the music quieted down and all heads turned in the direction of Easy, a hush slowly came over the crowd.

"I want to propose a toast to my man, Big C, and to his 19-year old son, CJ." I was just informed about his educational successes at school and I hear that he was recently awarded first place at the annual tristate chess tournament.

"I want everyone to grab a glass, because this round is on me."

The mere thought of a free round of drinks propelled everyone to gathered around the newly s- shaped curved bar and immediately Artie and Dee Dee began pouring the best chilled pink champagne in stock. The flow of free drinks from Easy Money had sparked a new enthusiasm in the crowd and Easy started his little speech.

"This is a toast to celebrate lifelong friendship, family ties, success, and continued movement forward into the future. This toast is to my good friends Big C, Anna and little CJ: May all your dreams and aspirations rise up to meet you with love."

"Ladies and gentlemen, let us all raise our glasses and give a hearty salute to Big C and his first-place son, CJ."

Easy Money led the crowd by slowly counting to three.

"One for the money, and two for the show, now three to get ready, let's go-go-go."

The crowd at Dee Dee's roared with a loud chanting three times: "Hip-hip-hooray and congratulations!"

The clinking of crystal glasses touching together was reminiscent of the sound of symbols coming from a drum set.

This was CJ's first time ever drinking any alcohol, at least in front of his father, so Carnell suggested that he drink it slowly. The two of them were having a good time and he just wanted to keep a keen eye open to ensure that his son wasn't over doing it.

As Carnell was smiling and admiring his son slowly sipping pink champagne he couldn't help to thinking what Anna would do to him if he brought his son home drunk. Anna rarely indulged in alcohol except for special occasions like Christmas or a wedding. She wasn't one to complain whenever Carnell made his once a week sojourn to Dee Dee's, and every now and then she'd accompany him just to talk to and be among friends.

The number of patrons that came over to greet and meet CJ seemed to be endless, but he managed to endure them all with patience and a warm smile. This was a special night of bonding between father and son and CJ was seeing a different side of his beloved community for the first time. He was loving every bit of it.

At a later time he would also recall that it felt as though he had discovered and embraced an extended family.

As CJ scanned the room, a trio of customers managed to get his complete attention. They were all beautiful and finely dressed. The one who seemed to be the leader was an older woman. She was accompanied by two other younger women of equally fine taste.

There was also a majestic presence about this trio that intrigued him far beyond their beauty. The woman elegantly positioned in the middle was gorgeous, Black, and of Caribbean descent. The beautiful woman to her right was White and of European descent. The third woman, positioned to her left. was stunningly tanned and of Asian descent. This trio of linked arms began to slowly and rhythmically walk toward him in an enticing manner. They were smiling and winking at CJ.

CJ felt excitement and fear all at the same time.

He hesitantly began to question his father as to who were these three women. Carnell turned toward them, chuckled, and said "That my boy is Betty McQueen.

She is the owner of the brothel that I pointed out to you earlier."

"Oh! So is that the Butterfly McQueen?"

"Yes, sir, in the flesh - and she's coming this way to meet you! I'll take care of this, just relax and remain calm."

"Hello, Calvin and CJ. It's not every day that I get to meet two handsome and virile young men sitting together."

"Hello Madame Butterfly. How are you this evening?"

"Thank you for asking, and, as you can see, we are all just fine."

The two other ladies spoke in unison while extending their hands for a delicately handshake to Carnell and CJ.

"It was my desire to come over and meet you for myself. Congratulations on your successes. You are now coming of age and you'll never know when, or if, you may ever need my services."

"Hopefully he won't!" said Big C in disgust.

"Ah, yes, but you'll never know until you do.

"Come along girls, these gentlemen don't need our services tonight."

The three of them slowly departed as strangely as they had appeared, but not before a glance back at CJ. With a giggle in their voices, they all said together: "Good bye CJ: we hope to see you around. Good night, Calvin, and please take good care of him."

CJ was sitting comfortably at the bar sipping his pink champagne and curiously surveying the joyous mood of the crowd when suddenly a heavy hand touched his shoulder and someone said to him, "Is it true that you are a champion chess player?"

CJ turned in the direction of the voice to see this small, White man who was wearing a tailored suit sporting a goatee and a well-trimmed moustache.

"Hi," he said, extending his hand to shake CJ's. "My name is, Sal Nardone, and I too play chess."

The two shook hands vigorously as CJ rose from his seat, offering it to the man to be seated next to his father.

Sal Nardone was a stable and important man within the community; he was also an active lieutenant of a prominent New Jersey mob family. It was his influence that made it possible for Artie and Dee Dee to receive a liquor license for the lounge. Everyone knew and respected his reputation for taking care of business, legal or otherwise. He was commonly known as Sal the Pal by his close, admiring friends.

To explain it more bluntly, Sal was the neighborhood watchman and he was the key to keeping away the pressure from any annoying politicians and police within the precincts of the Beehive. All of the business establishments in the 'Hive gladly paid him a monthly stipend for his services.

Sal was also an ardent player and student of the game of chess, having gained his superior skills when he was serving five years at a federal prison for the crimes of money laundering and extortion. While in the prison, he organized a chess club that garnered respect and praise from the governor and warden. He captained his team as they won several championships playing matches against competitors inside and out of the prison system.

"Oh," said Carnell; "I see the two of you have met."

"Yes, we have," said Sal.

"How are you, Mr. Carnell, and how is the Mrs.?"

It was his practice and a sign of respect to refer to all he spoke with as Mr. and Ms. If ever (if ever he referred to you by your first name, then you knew you were in for big trouble.)

"I thank you for asking. We are all just fine."

"That's a fine young lad you've got there, Mr. Carnell. Can I borrow him for a moment? I want to share something with him."

"Of course you can, Mr. Sal; I trust he's in good hands with you."

Carnell knew all about Sal's love of chess and had a good clue as to where they were going.

Sal turned toward CJ. He beckoned with his hands to follow him. The two of them began their navigation through the crowd to a quieter section of lounge located in the rear left corner.

Mr. Sal had built a unique alcove large enough for two tables and four people to play chess. The alcove was surrounded by soundproof glass and supported by two columns that served as an entrance. Inside this alcove two hanging globe lights were positioned over two very beautiful recessed tables; atop these tables were two custom- made marble boards and chess pieces. Inside the alcove were four arm chairs, two per table, that were also fashionably designed with firm cushioned backs and bottoms to provide comfort during long hours of a concentrated chess game.

The customers referred to this special section of the lounge as Mr. Sal's domain. He had it built when Artie and Dee Dee brought the lounge years ago. This was an exchange and a thank you to Mr. Sal for enabling them to receive their liquor license. It was also to ensure that Mr. Sal would always be close at hand for anything, at any time.

The very moment CJ entered this domain he was pleased and astonished; he had never seen a chess board and pieces so beautifully crafted.

"Wow, that's nice," said CJ, as he carefully examined the pieces and the boards. He was gently passing his hands over each piece as though they were precious stones, or some ancient artifact that he didn't want to damage.

"I've never seen anything like this before," said CJ.

"I had the entire set - the tables, chairs, and lights - all imported from Italy," said Sal, as CJ continued to explore the interior decor of the alcove.

"The game of chess is similar to the game of life. Every day the moves we make determine success or failure," Sal continued. "The difference between a good player and a great one is how to make moves and anticipate your opponent's moves in advance."

Every chess move has its consequences.

"I come here each day to unwind, think, and enjoy a good game of chess. It stimulates and prepares me for any important decisions or business transactions I may need to make."

Observing CJ's interest in the environment he had created for serious, competitive chess and sensing the young man's enthusiasm for the game, Sal asked,

"Perhaps if you have some idle time in the future, when you would care to join me for a game or some advance lessons."

The atmosphere within the alcove was enticing and CJ wanted to play right then and there. He didn't want to be rude and was trying to show politeness and patience to Mr. Sal; and so he said, "I would absolutely love that but, how do I get in touch with you?"

"Your father knows how to reach me, or I can leave a personal number at the front desk, with Mr. Artie and Mrs. Dee Dee," Sal replied.

Sal Nardone was a deep and quiet thinker and could size up most people in a matter of minutes.

As the night was passing and Big C was saying goodnight and thanking everyone, Sal caught up with him.

"Mr. Carnell, your son is a unique young man. He is a thinker, he is courteous, and he is respectful. And I believe he has a bright future, and will do great things in this city." he said.

"I hope you don't mind, but we are planning to play one another, and I will be his mentor and coach so I can hopefully improve his game."

Carnell was impressed and proud to hear this kind of insight from Mr. Sal, after such a short interview with his son. He smiled broadly and said, "Thank you very much, but I warn you he is a precise and deliberate player."

"I can tell," Sal remarked, "but so am I, so am I."

These two well-known men of the community embraced each other with a hug and loving salutations for their respective families, then bid one another goodnight.

"I will be looking forward to playing you very soon," Sal said to CJ.

"It will be my honor," said CJ, "and I hope I can learn much from you."

Time always passes quickly when you're having fun, and so it was for CJ having his first drink and open invitation to Dee Dee's Lounge. He was feeling mature and secure in the company of so many adults, some of whom were important and some not so much. The best feeling however came from spending quality time with his father respectfully and being treated equally.

The educational tour the two had taken through the Beehive had left an indelible effect upon him, the likes of which he would never forget. This evening would forever be remembered as intriguing and exciting, with new acquaintances, introductions, and lofty expectations for the future. This night had enabled Charles to grow more aware of his city, his father, and the open possibilities that lay ahead for him.

The time was now 10:45 and the lounge was becoming crowded with folks who love to stay out late. The patrons were having a grand time dancing, drinking, and laughing.

"Okay son, I guess I better start getting you home. Did you have a nice time and how are you feeling?"

"I had a wonderful time and I'm feeling just fine. I'm ready whenever you are."

CJ helped his father with his coat and hat and then began heading toward the door. As they stepped through the doorway, they were greeted by Bootsy, who was just arriving and determined to be there until closing time.

"The party is going on behind you, so where are you two going?"

"Well, it's getting late for my son, so we are on our way home."

"Oh, is this your son? It's nice to meet you. My name is Bootsy."

When CJ heard that name he remembered the story about those

infamous boots laced with sharpened metal. Sure enough, they were pointed alligator boots with gold metal wrapped around the front ends. He couldn't help thinking about the costly damage that those razor-sharp boots could do to human flesh.

"Where are you parked? I didn't see your car out front."

"I'm parked about four blocks away on Johnson Avenue."

"Allow me to give you a lift. I just arrived and I'll be here for a while. And you don't want to walk through all that traffic on the streets tonight."

"Are you sure?" replied Carnell. "I don't want to put you out of your way."

"It's no problem; I'm right at the curb. Get in please."

"OK thanks a lot - we appreciate the lift."

As father and son entered the car, CJ realized it was the same Jaguar they had witnessed while they were strolling slowly down Broadway. On the drive back toward where they were parked, the duo was witnessed the activities on the streets that Carnell had pointed out earlier in the evening. The crowds had increased twofold and yet it was only 11:30, an early hour for the long nights at the Beehive.

The conversation heading home was memorable for both Carnell and his son. They had shared an evening filled with history, excitement, and much love.

When they arrived at home, Anna was soundly asleep in bed and Carnell made haste to join her.

CJ didn't go to bed for a while; the scenes and conversations he had experienced were too fresh to put out of mind.

As he lay in bed looking up at the ceiling he could visualize the places and all the people that his father pointed out for him. The resounding and echoing words from his father kept repeating in his head and he replayed them over and over again.

"I urge you to be smart, stay alert, and avoid the Beehive. This is not for you, and I expect you to do better.

"Remember your education is the key to unlocking your dreams."

The Beehive section of town was historic and had expanded over the decades, and yet it remained a pivotal component of daily life in the city. In spite of the years of lawless activities involving various types of vice, this area continued to thrive and grow.

CJ kept thinking to himself that there was one steady and constant common denominator to all of this: the money. The supply and demand for vice and the profits that poured in as a result enabled a small network of people to always benefit.

CJ was remembering reading novels about crimes and the life of criminals in history and the repeated message that crime doesn't pay. The events he had experience this night gave him cause to doubt that message, and he now was beginning to think that it did pay. Shortly before he readied himself for a long night's sleep' he recorded in his daily journal a detailed account of what he had learned - to keep as a reminder and a direction to consider as he was entering a new era of his life.

After recording some notes of importance, he said a small prayer thanking God for guiding them safely back to their home. The last thing he remembered before falling asleep was to glance at the two phone numbers he received from Mr. Sal; he was thinking about if and when they would play a game of chess in the comforts of that beautiful alcove.

Loving thoughts of his girlfriend Cynthia and the stories he would share concerning this night formed the potion that finally put his mind to rest. He began quietly wondering what her possible reactions would be, and he could hardly wait to see and be with her to share the sights he had seen and the lessons he had learned this special night. Finally he softly said, "Here's good night to you, my love. God willing, I shall see you tomorrow."

CHAPTER 7

The heartbreak

S unday mornings and Sunday breakfast in the kitchen of the Sinclair house were specifically reserved for reflections on the previous week and projections for the next. Anna would prepare a delicious breakfast for her two men and the three of them would come together to the kitchen table praising God, and then they would discuss concerns or issues during the past week.

Normally Anna would talk about the women's auxiliary she belonged to and their recent or projected community activities. She had been a member for more than a decade now and her fellow members had elected her to the office of regional secretary. Anna enjoyed being active and she was vigilant about community service for the sick, destitute, and those in the greatest need. She had a loving and giving heart and there was always something for her to assist with or involve her fellow members.

Often times you could hear her say, "If you want to get, then you have to give." Another of her favorite quotes was, "Service to humanity is service to God."

She was mindful of her youthful days in Cuba and the experience of poverty that she once lived. Her heart was filled with gratitude to God for her marriage to Carnell, for coming to America, and for being a mother to Charles. On this Sunday she was eager to share some news with the two loves of her life.

"Guess what, guys? The mayor is issuing us a proclamation for our community service." Our group has contributed record amounts of money and other help to support the sick and shut-in, feed the hungry, and for the coats and blankets drive of this past winter. We have been selected as the number one voluntary community service group in the city. And the mayor will present the proclamation to me as secretary of the Ladies Auxiliary - and our picture will be shown in the daily newspaper.

"Isn't that some great news?"

'Wow!" exclaimed Carnell, "that's fantastic news."

Charles had come to the kitchen table as usual with his head buried into a book; but upon the hearing this news, he looked up with a broad smile and said, "That is great news and I'm so proud of you, Mom."

Next it was Carnell's turn to reflect and share, and so he began, "I am proud to announce that I have received the honor and title of employee of the month, and I have received a raise of 75 cent per hour extra in my weekly paycheck.

"And let me announce to my darling wife that the trip you wanted to Cuba is now closer at hand, and with this extra money we can now more easily afford to go. How would you like to leave in June after CJ's graduation?"

"I would love to go, honey, at any time you suggest."

Anna and Carnell hugged each other and shared a passionate kiss.

They then turned to CJ and asked, "Do you have anything to share with us? How are you and Cynthia? And what may I ask are you reading?"

"Cynthia and I are just fine and I am trying to finish reading a novel about the life and times of the infamous gangster, Al Capone."

It didn't alarm Anna or Carnell that he was reading these types of books; they had always encouraged him to simply read, enjoy, and learn. CJ was a regular reader of all kinds of books covering a vast array of subjects. If one were to categorize his reading habits, chess strategies and gambits would be first and books concerning the life of gangsters during the roaring '20s and beyond would be second.

"Well, son, are you learning anything from it?"

"As a matter of fact, yes, I am. I've learned that if he were smarter and more aware of the primary principles of mathematics he probably would have never gone to prison. After all, it was his stubborn accountant who was caught by the government that thrust him into trouble.

"I also read that before he reached the age of 28 he became a multi-millionaire and owner of vast properties. I think it is ironic that he too ruled over an empire that resembles many of the same activities that occur in the Beehive.

"To many immigrant people during those times he was considered to be a hero and an example of how to rise out of poverty," CJ concluded.

It was CJ's emphasis on the word poverty that got his father's attention and so he said, "Yes, that is true. But it is also a fact that he broke the law continuously and had many people murdered as he made those millions of dollars. I know you don't think that breaking the law is the only way out of poverty, do you?"

Carnell paused for a moment then made the suggestion, "Sometimes money can be the root of all evil."

"Ah, yes; but he was never convicted of any of those alleged crimes. He was supplying a service that the people wanted and in turn providing jobs."

All Carnell could do about that response was to nod his head in agreement and reply; "That was spoken like a true lover of math and a chess competitor."

Anna and Carnell looked at their intelligent son and appeared surprised that he admired a person who was considered to be public enemy number one by the United States government.

They just chuckled and the three continued enjoying their Sunday breakfast.

I'm going to church this morning," Anna said. "Are either of you going to join me?"

"No thank you my dear. I'm going to relax today and watch some television."

"Thanks, Mom, for asking, but I'm hoping to visit Cynthia and her grandmother today. I haven't seen either of them in a few days."

"OK, guys. Can you at least clean up the kitchen and wash the dishes?"

"Sure, love, we can do that. I'll wash them and CJ can dry and put them away."

"I'll see you two after the Sunday services."

Anna went to get dressed. Returning shortly, she kissed her loving husband and son and left for church.

The Sinclair family firmly believed in the one supreme God, but going to church every week wasn't a ritual they indulged in as a family. The specific times they regularly attended church together were Easter Sunday, Mother's Day, and New Year's Eve.

Carnell and CJ quietly remained at the table, in sync with the slow minute hand movements of the clock on the yellow kitchen wall. It was Big C's daily habit to thoroughly read the local newspaper and then search through the sports page to check for the winning numbers of the day. CJ kept his head buried in his book, engrossed in the history of Al Capone. Every few minutes during his reading there issued a grunting sound followed by, "I would have done that differently;" or "that wasn't a smart move."

That is who CJ was - constantly analyzing, planning, and calculating his next two or three moves. His parents didn't fully understood at the time, but CJ was subconsciously applying tactical movements of chess for everyday situations to his life.

Whenever Carnell heard these low grunting sounds, he simply looked up from the paper, smiled, and then shook his head. He realized it wasn't necessary for him to comment or disturb their contentment. It was quite evident that this time together was serving as a refuge and a reminder that silence is truly golden.

It was after 1 o'clock when CJ decided to telephone Cynthia. He thought she and her grandmother would be home from church by then and he would ask to come by for a visit.

It was the middle of May and nature was adorned in beautiful arrangements of colors and smells, and the relationship between CJ and Cynthia was blossoming like a new spring flower. The two of them were becoming inseparable. They were one of the most admired and popular couples, enjoying each other's company and always on the go.

They shared mutual interests in nature, walks, reading novels, laughing together, and they often attended a movie or two at the local cinema. Cynthia had become the only person who could come between Charles and his best friend, O'Neil. And although they would remain best friends for life, they both understood the important effects of a female being central in their young lives. There were special times when they would go out on a double date in order to stay connected. Fortunately for CJ, those were the times that he'd be experience love from two of the most important peers in his life.

CJ borrowed the car from his father and drove the scenic route to Cynthia's home with full anticipation of spending time with both her and the grandmother - a tender and wise woman who admired CJ and his fondness of her only grandchild - and she preferred that he call her Nana. The warmth, wisdom, and unconditional love from a grandparent were things that CJ had never known before; he had lost both his grandparents early in his childhood. He looked forward to any time he could share in her company and he cherished the relationship between her and Cynthia.

Upon his arrival he carefully parked the Chevrolet in the driveway of the upscale split-level home then rang the bell three times. It was starting to rain steadily as he patiently stood at the door expecting either of them to answer. When he got no response he rang the bell three more times.

It was Cynthia who finally answered the door, albeit without her normal happy response. She desperately made an attempt to hide the fact that something was wrong, but CJ saw through the façade and said, "Hi babe, are you all right? What' the matter?"

"Hi, CJ," she said, barely looking at him and holding her head held down.

He could see evidence of half-wiped tears upon her face and he instantly knew there was a problem. He found himself still standing in the doorway like a stranger.

"May I come in? Where is Nana?"

Cynthia slowly moved aside, barely looking at him. CJ came in, grabbed her hand, and headed for the sofa to sit and get some answers.

"Nana has fallen asleep, but I have something very frightening to share with you."

"Sure, honey, what is it?"

CJ took out a handkerchief from his sport jacket pocket and began wiping her eyes to reinforce that he was there for her. Cynthia looked up at him with saddened eyes and said, "The reason I haven't talked with you for a few days is because of Nana's health. She was complaining of chest pains and I took her to the doctors for an examination. The doctor took blood samples from her, and then he ran some more tests, only to conclude that she has malignant tumors in her breast."

A look of shock and worry appeared on his face and hesitantly he questioned, "What does that all mean?"

Once again the tears began to gently fall from those lovely brown eyes

of using these two strong principles together is what marks the difference between winning and losing.

Cynthia was surprised and impressed admiring this piece of jewelry, and ironically the pearls matched a set of earrings she once received from her Nana.

CJ's explanation, however, meant more to her than the jewelry itself.

"This is the most thoughtful gift I have ever received," she said, "and this is why I love you."

The two held each other tightly, and, before holding back tears, kissed affectionately.

"We better get ready for the trip to the airport," reminded CJ, "I'm going home to change clothes and my mother and father said they would drive to see you off."

It was Anna's idea for CJ to purchase the necklace. It had not dawned on her before the death of Nana just how much her son really loved Cynthia. She jealously wanted to see the necklace worn around Cynthia's neck and to take a Kodak picture of them together for her photo albums.

The ride to the airport seemed longer than normal and it was noticeably quiet. Carnell suggested to not linger longer than needed because it would only lengthen the pain. The morgue from Carver Hospital had already boarded the casket for Nana and there was nothing left to do but kiss, hug, and say goodbyes. As Cynthia was about to board the plane she turned for one last time, blowing a kiss to her adopted family and bidding them what would be her last goodbye.

The ride back home was a dreary and lonely one for CJ and he contemplated the meaning of recent events and how they related to his future. Upon arrival at home he went to his room for meditation and silent prayer, asking God for understanding and guidance.

It was very difficult trying to relax or remove Cynthia from his mind at the time and so he decided that perhaps a good book might do the trick. After reading a lengthy paragraph or two he realized it wasn't working and he began looking for Mr. Sal's phone numbers. Playing the game of chess had always been stimulating and relaxing for him, so his desire was to find and engage Sal for a game.

CJ placed a call to Dee Dee's Lounge and fortunately was able to located Sal.

Sal was glad to hear from him and invited him to come and join him for a game or two. Dee Dee's Lounge generally opened at noon and closed at 3 o'clock in the morning. Since CJ was on spring break from school and it was a Thursday afternoon, he expected that the lounge wouldn't be very crowded.

He promptly got into his car and headed to Dee Dee's Lounge to meet and play Mr. Sal. The lounge looked much different from his initial visit. There were no crowds of people and he could see its entirety unobscured.

Sal was sitting at the bar and welcomed him to join him.

"What would you like to drink?" asked Sal.

"I'll have a club soda, thank you."

"That's a good choice," Sal replied.

The two of them engaged in small talk for a while before proceeding to the alcove. As CJ entered, he surveyed the alcove. It was as beautiful and inviting as he remembered. The tension of Cynthia's departure that had engulfed him earlier was starting to ease as the two took their respective seats at the chess table.

"Shall I flip a coin for which color you'd like?"

"Sure," replied CJ.

Sal took a quarter from his pocket and said; "I choose heads for black and you can have white if it's tails."

"OK," said CJ. "That's fine with me."

The coin turned up tails and CJ took the opportunity to make the first move. It was the classical first move, E4.

Sal followed with a typical Sicilian defense of c5.

The game was intense as both players carefully calculated each move toward an anticipated victory. The first game lasted for more than an hour, with Sal being awarded the win. The second game was equally as vigorous and long and resulted with CJ winning impressively.

"That was a good game," said Sal. "I was impressed with your defense. What was it?"

"That was a French defense. I was forced to switch from a center counter defense because of your offensive skills."

Sal could tell that CJ had studied chess thoroughly and was a true student of the game. He respected players who studied the masters of the game; he knew that it was the only formula for success.

The two discontinued playing for a while and Sal began to have an open conversation, asking how his studies were progressing and what were his favorite subjects in school. CJ talked earnestly about why mathematics was his favorite course of study. He referred mathematics as being the highest level of thinking for problem solving and how it reminding him of unlimited chess maneuvers. He also mentioned that he received straight A's in geometry and calculus.

The second on his list of favorite subjects, he said, was history, because it was the one subject that rewarded his research.

Sal was an intelligent man and had great respect for those who possessed intelligence as well. He was primarily intrigued about the thought processes of CJ's young mind as he had observed his focused thinking while playing the game of chess.

"Please tell me, what do you do for social life? Do you have a girlfriend? And how about work - do you have a job?"

These questions seemed to momentarily catch CJ off guard, but he regained his composure, took a deep breath and then answered, "Yes, I do have a girlfriend, but unfortunately her grandmother recently passed away and today she flew back to California to live with her parents.

"I am currently working at the sports trophy store on Prince Street."

"Is that what was on your mind during our first game?" This question surprised CJ and for a moment his mind shifted back to thoughts of Cynthia.

"I noticed you seemed to be out of focus. I thought you should have won the first game; you were much more focused during our second game."

At that moment CJ realized that Sal was not just playing a friendly game of chess, but rather he was studying him.

"I have a proposal for you, Mr. Charles. How would you like to have a job using your mathematic skills? I have a relative who owns an accounting firm and he is looking for some new employees who have bright minds, such as you."

"I would absolutely love such an opportunity."

"I'm glad to hear that you see it as an opportunity."

"I do," CJ replied. "I was taught by my father and mother that if offered any opportunity to improve yourself you should take it and make the best of it."

"I agree, and I will put forth a letter of introduction and set up the interview with my cousin Vinney Nardone, and then you can go from there."

A wide smile appeared on CJ's face and his heart was bursting with thanks and gratitude. He wanted desperately to find a higher paying job and independently take responsibility for the various expenses associated with his upcoming prom and graduation. He realized that Calvin and Anna would bear the cost of anything he needed, but this was a matter of pride that he had to prove to himself.

"I don't know how to thank you, Mr. Sal; I'm so honored and grateful. I thank you once again, one thousand times over."

"You can thank me by taking this opportunity and working hard to make it grow far beyond anyone's expectations."

"I can do that with God's help," replied CJ.

As the hours quickly passed, CJ was surprised that he talked to Mr. Sal openly without reservation or judgment; and he thoroughly enjoyed that feeling.

"Do you have time for one more game?"

"I sure do. Do you want heads or tails?"

The bigger and more important strategy that Sal was engaged in was mentorship. He had for years painstakingly searched for the right person to teach and encourage - an individual who wasn't arrogant, cocky, or hot-headed. Sal was an astute professional and in his line of work trust and accountability are the most valued assets one can have; they can either make you or break you.

It had to be someone who wasn't a family member or felt they had an inherited right to entitlement. He needed a young man with intelligence and calculating skills - someone who could visualize situations and find working solutions before problems actually materialized.

Mr. Sal Nardone had developed a unique empire that employed many people with a vested interest in promoting trade and commerce. In other words, he had the products that people wanted and he controlled the flow of them. He wasn't the godfather and overseer of the Beehive for nothing; it was because he made the right decisions at the right times and with the right people.

Sal realized from the first introduction that CJ had a seasoned quality about him and a certain maturity that was rare in most people his age. He exuded a discipline and manner of calm confidence. Sal had concluded that after years of searching and yearning to coach or mentor a protégé, that very person was now sitting right in front of him. A healthy seedpod was being planted to produce his successor to the multi-million dollar empire, and what he needed now was to fertilize, nurture, and reap the benefits.

Sal had been looking over the chess board for a couple of minutes before he proclaimed, "I've had enough chess for today, young man; this one is a stalemate."

"Yes; I agree, and my brain is worn out as well."

They both rose from their chairs, stretching and yawning as they left the alcove.

"I'll get started on that letter of recommendation tomorrow and I'll contact you in a day or two. Is that alright?"

"Sure, that's perfectly fine with me. And let me express my appreciation for your time and attention this afternoon I know you are a busy man and I am indebted to you and wish to express my thankfulness."

"You are quite the chess player, CJ, and I look forward to some return matches in the very near future."

'Thank you, sir, and have a good night."

As CJ was heading toward his car he smiled and thought to himself about the good fortune that had just occurred. He had played a tough competitor with one loss, one victory, and one ultimate tied score. He had discovered another outlet for himself while establishing good ties with a chess advisor or a possible new friend.

The greatest victory for him was the prospect of a new job with an accounting firm and the possibility of making more money. He could hardly wait to share the great news with his parents. After all, when they last saw him he was sad and depressed.

The day had started out with feelings of agony and hurt as Cynthia boarded a plane for distant California, but had ended with encouragement and feelings of harmony and hope from his visit with Mr. Sal.

Suddenly there was light tapping on the window as he started the car, and to his amazement there stood Sal with a newspaper in his hand. CJ quickly let down the window and Sal said, "I understand you are an avid reader and I wanted to give you something of interest to read."

"What is it?" asked CJ as he pondered how Sal knew of his reading habits.

"It's The Wall Street Journal and in it is some good math information concerning stocks and bonds. Why don't you check it out for yourself?"

"Thank you again, and I surely will read it tonight before I get to sleep."

"Good night, CJ."

Once again here was Sal the Pal Nardone anticipating and planting seeds - ever the consummate chess player, forever initiating the first movement toward a strategic victory.

CHAPTER 8

Beyond heartbreak

Sitting at his desk surrounded by his many chess trophies, CJ could refresh his emotions, body, and spirit. In this special place he could meditate, read, reflect, and then prepare to take on the responsibilities of the day. This was his sanctuary - off limits to others - where he could exhale and release whatever had driven him there in the first place.

It had been more than a year and a half since Cynthia had moved to California, and although they continued to write, the letters were becoming more and more infrequent. There were multiple and legitimate reasons for the distractions that existed between them. Chief among them was that she now attended the University of Southern California and he was receiving promotions at the accounting firm that committed him to wider responsibilities and occupied more of his time.

He also was fast-tracking into an evening MBA program at a nearby branch of Rutgers University. Both he and Cynthia were maturing, growing, and meeting different kinds of people, and responding to opportunities that presented themselves daily.

The last letter that he received from Cynthia, dated April 25, 1976, was not a positive one.

The letter was filled with praise for their long-time friendship and recalled all kinds of memorial dates from the places and times gone by. She wrote with such distinction and descriptive style that CJ felt the full emotional impact of every word. Her letter had left nothing unsaid and included such intimate details as their first enchanted French kiss and the first time she uttered the words, "I love you."

It was the conclusion her this letter that confounded CJ the and left him completely perplexed. Cynthia wrote that she would continue to have love and respect for him, but that she would be moving on and investing her time with other people. After stating that she planned to permanently separate, she coldly suggested that he do the same.

CJ read those unwelcome words of advice several times before noticing something wrapped in red tissue paper.

He began to nervously open the package, only to discover that it was the friendship and connection necklace that he had given her before she left for California.

On the day he received the letter, CJ sat his desk, staring at both the letter and the necklace for what could have been hours. He was deeply hurt and couldn't understand why it had to be this way.

In his heart, he had felt that time and distance would be something he'd conquer and eventually overcome. He was an eternal optimist who always saw the glass as half full and never empty. It took some time for him to digest and fully understand that his first love relationship was over.

There followed many deep conversations with his mother that helped him comprehend the difference in thinking patterns between men and women. Time was what he needed to heal, but the experience of losing Cynthia left a scar that would remain with him indefinitely.

Four months later, while CJ was sitting at his desk, he began to shift his focus toward the up-coming celebration of his 21st birthday. He hadn't made any definite plans as yet and was contemplating how he wanted to handle it. There was one thought however that kept hounding him and it was the fact he was still a virgin. He had never imagined the possibility of being intimate with any female other than Cynthia.

The haunting reality of her absence had now begun to percolate in his head. He thought about having this conversation with his father but was too embarrassed to follow through. He decided a plausible alternative for such a sensitive conversation would be to go to Mr. Sal.

One day while playing one of their weekly competitive chess matches, CJ felt confident enough to talk with Sal about his dilemma. The second match had concluded and their routine was to sit in between matches and talk candidly about issues or concerns of the day. CJ began by asking Sal, "I was wondering if I may ask you a personal question."

"Sure thing, you can ask me anything you like; just be ready for the answer."

"How old were you when you broke your virginity?"

"Well, that is very personal. I recall the first female that I made love with was older than me, and I think I was 16 or 17 at the time. Why do you ask?"

"Do you remember me speaking with you about the young lady who was my first love, Cynthia?"

Sal slowly nodded his head in agreement but still had a puzzled expression on his face.

"Please continue," he said.

After taking a deep breath to re-focus, CJ decided to come to the point.

"We recently broke up and she has been the only female I have been somewhat intimate with, or ever wanted to be. My birthdate is coming at the end of October and I will be 21 years of age and technically I'm still a virgin. I have kissed and fondled her on many past occasions, but we never went all the way. My body and mind are telling me it's time, but I don't have a girlfriend and don't know what to do."

Sal looked at CJ as if he was a concerned father about to give good advice.

"That's nothing to be ashamed or embarrassed about and it's a minor concern that can easily be remedied. I appreciate you talking to me about this matter; after all you are handsome, strong, and intelligent and I'm confident that this small problem can be corrected."

Despite the shyness he often projected, his popularity was soaring. He had a well-paying, respectable job, owned a nice car, and dressed very well. The truth is that CJ had plenty of admirers he could have dated, but his heart was still captured by Cynthia, and now she was permanently gone.

Sal was looking at CJ while smiling to himself before he asked, "When exactly is your birthdate?"

"It's October 31, on Halloween."

"Do you want a trick or a treat? And have you ever been on a blind date?"

"No, I haven't and I'll take a treat any day; I've had far too many tricks lately."

"Anything is possible," said Sal. "Be patient a little longer and it'll all work out."

"I may as well be; after all it's been 20 years already; a few more days couldn't possibly hurt."

"I agree; let's set up the pieces for one more game."

As they began to play their third game of the day, Sal made a mental note on how he would solve this problem for his young protégé. He knew exactly who to contact and he was very confident his idea would make the perfect birthday treat at for CJ. at Halloween.

The separation, time, and distance between CJ and Cynthia had become a catalyst for his personal growth and discipline.

The two celebratory events nearing the end of his senior year were sacrificed. He had not attended his high school prom despite his friend O'Neil making arrangements with girls who desired to be his date. During the time of his senior graduation he felt sorrowful despite the many awards he received; it just was not the same without Cynthia there.

At times his focus waned to the point wherein he became moody or despondent. He was not in a very happy state of mind and even his passion for chess dropped to a level of discontent - except when he played against Sal. He was, however, now determined to leave those sorrowful times behind him as he looked toward a new beginning - starting with his 21st birthday celebration.

The end of October was drawing near and during a weekly game played with Mr. Sal he was given an envelope with an address and instructions as to what he should do on the 31st day of October. CJ opened the unsealed envelope, read it and agreed to follow the detailed instructions from Mr. Sal. He had already contacted the infamous Madame Butterfly to explain the dilemma of his protégé before prepaying for CJ's appointment. He further gave clear instructions for her best lady to give CJ a night filled with exotic and lustful pleasures beyond his wildest imagination.

As October ends, it marks the beginning of a seasonal change from fall to winter throughout the northeastern section of the United States. There is a slight chill in the air that prepares and introduces the change to a winter that is sure to come.

The date of Halloween reflects an additional change beyond the sequential seasons.

It is also a change from everyday clothing to costumes, donned for the exchange of candy and treats for the simple ringing of a doorbell or the pounding of a neighbor's door, which may lead to shouting, "trick or treat."

That year the festive holiday of Halloween and CJ's birthdate would fall on a Thursday, which meant there would be less traffic of kids and adults seeking treats or tricks.

As he arrived home from work he was greeted by the singing of "Happy Birthday" and a few small gifts from his mom and dad. As always, CJ showed his gratitude and then thank them with hugs and kisses.

"I can't believe you're going to be 21 years old," said Carnell.

"My baby is going to be legally a grown man," Anna added. "I remember that stormy night on Halloween 21 years ago."

"Yes," said Carnell, "and praise the Lord you made it all right and you have been all right ever since."

"Do you have any plans for this evening?"

"Well, I know there are a few parties around town; so I thought I might hang out with the boys for a while."

"OK. Have fun and be careful - there are a lot of crazies out there tonight."

"I will and thanks for the gifts. I love you both, you're the greatest."

CJ headed to his room and immediately began his mental preparation for his scheduled appointment of the night. On his dresser he noticed the white envelope he had received from Mr. Sal and he began to wonder about its contents. He had honored his promised not to look inside, and he assured Sal that he would be at 1252 Broadway at 8 p.m. that evening.

He was somewhat perplexed when he noticed the envelope was addressed to Ms. Betty. He did not make the mental connection at that time as to who she was.

The time was approaching 6 o'clock and he had plenty of time to unwind a bit, take a shower, and then get himself ready.

Charles was always disciplined with his time management and rarely late to any appointment. He decided to give enough time to observe the children going about their frolicking routines of trick and treating, remembering how it was as a child not too many years ago.

As he drove up to the address he was surprised to learn that it was the Cut and Curl hair and beauty salon that his father had pointed out to him almost two years ago. Initially he envisioned himself sitting to receive a stylish haircut, but then thought about the timeframe; he just couldn't imagine what was in store for him.

When he entered the highly fashionable place of business, he was greeted by a beautiful woman, who smilingly said,

"Good evening, how can I help you?"

"I have an 8 clock appointment," said CJ as he reached inside his sport jacket and handed her the envelope addressed to Ms. Betty.

"Please have a seat and I will get her right away."

CJ promptly took a seat looking around and admiring the elegantly dressed people sitting in salon chairs. A minute or two passed before a short-statured woman walked toward him and politely said, "Good evening, CJ. I'm pleased to see you made it on time."

As he looked up he remembered seeing this face before, and then he realized it was none other than the infamous Madame Butterfly McQueen.

"Happy birthday," she said. "We have a lovely treat for you this evening.

"If you would just follow me, there is a men's room to your right with a bathrobe and towel awaiting you; you can strip down to your shorts and put on the robe. After you undress there is a red button near the sink; please press the button. A door will open that leads you to the second floor. Your room is 201.

"Just relax and enjoy your birthday gift."

At first he was surprised to learn that she knew about his birthday, and then he realized that this was possibly all arranged by Sal. Charles was somewhat nervous. Everything was happening so fast, and besides he was a little shy. But he managed to catch his breath and proceeded with her directions.

Room 201 was dimly lit with a blue lights and classical jazz music was softly playing, piped in from two speakers placed on opposite sides of the small room.

A delightful scent of lavender permeated the air, giving the room a relaxed yet sensuous feeling of more to come.

Occupying the room was a queen size bed covered by a mauve satin sheet that was strewn with rose petals. Fluffy pillows were stacked against the dark wood headboard. A chaise lounge was artfully placed nearby. He sat down upon the lounge chair in contemplated what would follow next.

In a few minutes there was soft knocking at the door and a small astonishingly beautiful Asian woman entered the room singing the traditional "Happy Birthday" song. She was stunningly dressed, wearing a red silk negligee outfit and black silk stockings. A yellow flower was tucked neatly into her long, flowing black hair.

"Good evening, my name is Mia - and you must be Charles. Or should I call you CJ?"

"You can call me CJ - that would be just fine."

His head was now spinning because he had never seen any woman dressed like this, except those he remembered in Playboy magazines.

She walked toward him and whispered into his ear, "I am your birthday present and I will fulfill your most seductive delights for the next two hours."

She reached for his hand and gently guided him to the awaiting bed. It was obvious that CJ's nerves were jumping out of control, but, being a seasoned professional, she proceeded to relax him with soft touches and soothing words.

As they moved closer to the bed, she slowly removed her negligee and stockings and stood completely naked before him with her legs straddled, giving him time to observe her petite, luscious body inch by inch. She gently began guiding him onto the bed, carefully removing his bathrobe and his shorts.

After CJ had fully observed Mia's nakedness, he marveled at the manner in which her long black hair was draping her breast, the smoothness of her thighs and protruding buttocks. It had taken him 21 years to witness the beauty and structure of a woman's body and he felt it was worth every year of waiting.

She mounted her small frame on to his thighs, facing him with widened eyes, so as to give him a closer look and smell from her body.

The sweet smell of her perfume was intoxicating and as she began kissing and nibbling at his navel, his eyes rolled back, his head tilted sideways, and low-toned moaning flowed from his opened mouth.

She was now roaming toward his chest muscles, kissing ever so passionately with the fullest intentions of reaching his inviting lips. At last she reached for his head with both small hands. Their mouths met with wet tongues thrusting and traveling over each other, intent on finding their open, moist mouths.

Her body was warm and moist. She beckoned CJ to slowly run his fingers through her hair and explore all the beautiful curves of her perfectly shaped body.

The rhythmic massaging and kissing continued until she felt his thigh muscles tightening and his penis growing firm and wet beyond his control. In her most provocative voice she called out his name over and over again, as her head moved toward his hardening penis. Suddenly she grabbed the long, hot, hardened penis with moist hands and thrust it into her awaiting saliva filled mouth.

CJ's body reacted immediately. He jerked up as if he were struck by a lightning. To his amazement, he began to express himself with long and loud curses.

"Oh shit," he exclaimed. "That felt so damn good."

Hearing those exciting and encouraging words from an inexperienced lover only served to intensify her efforts as she stroked and sucked with open abandonment. They were both sweating profusely and the passions were heightening with every movement and with ever groan.

"I want and need your strong cock inside of me," she uttered with new intensity.

At that moment she climbed atop him and measured with her hand the thickness and length of his warm manhood before thrusting it inside her vagina. Her moaning was long, loud, and intense as she began to ride his hard penis.

CJ instinctively wrapped his hands around her tender body as he changed positions and now was atop her. She spread open her legs as wide as possible and he began his long, determined thrusting in, out, and around her vagina. They were chanting and moaning one another's names with pure ecstasy and delight.

She pleaded for him to squeeze her ass tightly while she wrapped her legs around his back and pulled him ever closer into her pulsating body before crying out, "I want you to please take me, take all of this sweet pussy."

"Yes," screamed CJ; "I want every inch of you."

The ecstatic breathing gave way to new positioning and he obliged her by turning her over and placing her so that she was on bending knees. She put her head down and arched her back to receive his cock. All of the muscles in his body began to expand with strength, enabling him to drive his throbbing erection deeper into her. The intensity of this youthful, strong, controlled thrusting caused her to scream with joy the repeated cries of, "Yes. Yes." and "Please, baby, please."

CJ's hot body was gyrating harder than ever now and sweat was pouring out from all over him. He started feeling something new, and, strangely, Mia was feeling it, too. He was steadying his erection for a full ejaculation inside her hot and moist vagina, when suddenly she looked back at him, begging him to wait, so they could do it together. He was pulling her hair from behind and some most unusual curse words were coming forth with no control.

He continued to thrust and grind as deeply as possible into her now limp body, inch by hard inch, and then there was the flowing explosion of warm semen pouring into her pussy. Mia was jerking her body uncontrollably as she gratefully received all that was emitting from that black dick.

He was holding her tightly and trying to breathe normally, but it was impossible.

The two slowly collapsed onto the sweat-soaked sheets. As he rolled off of her they both turned onto their backs with arms and legs limp from pure exhaustion and stared up at the ceiling.

"That was amazing," said CJ.

He didn't dare reveal that it was his first time, and all he desired at that moment was to breathe and calm down.

"I enjoyed you very much," Mia said as she removed herself from the bed and reached for a nearby towel to dry him off.

"There is a sink and a fresh wash cloth for you, if you wish to freshen up a bit."

"Thank you," he said, but he was too tired to move right away. He just wanted to soak in the fantastic experience or wake up from what seemed like an improbable dream.

Mia looked at the clock on the wall and realized that the two hours were about to end, so she gracefully gathered her things and started to leave. It had been awhile since she made love with such a strong, tender, and young man and she definitely couldn't remember if it was ever done with a virgin before.

Madame Butterfly had told her of Sal's plan to go easy on him, but the reverse had happened to her and she thoroughly enjoyed every minute.

She walked toward CJ whispering to him that she hoped he enjoyed his birthday gift; then she kissed him on the lips, bidding him a restful, sweet goodnight.

"You will find your clothes upon a bench outside of this room," she said.

CJ took one long lasting glance at her nakedness as she tip-toed toward the light switch to turn off the blue lights and switch on the green. It was her signal that his time had expired and he should prepare himself to leave. He sat up and readied himself from the sprawled-out position to a vertical one, retrieved his clothing, and walked out of room 201.

He decided to take the scenic route home along Broadway so he could observe the night's activities of the Beehive and continue a thoughtful reprise of the experiences he had shared with Mia.

Upon his arrival home he prepared himself to take a long, hot, and soapy shower and then climb into bed. He was fully exhausted but relieved by the thoughts he would treasure and relieved to no longer be a virgin. As he lay in his comfortable bed he continued to savor the scent of Mia's perfume and hear the sultry whispers of her Asian accent, still very present in his mind. It took a while for him to fall off to sleep as his mind would replay the vivid scenes of his initiation to making love.

As he turned on his side, adjusting his position, he could hardly wait to see and thank Mr. Sal for a wonderful birthday celebration. The last thing he remembered before drifting to sleep was the repeated utterance of gratitude.

"Thank you, Mia," he said, "thank you."

The very next day CJ awoke with a revitalized spirit. The accounting firm had given him the day off and he looked forward to having a three-day weekend to completely unwind and relax. He was planning to share some quality time with his friend O'Neil. Their crushing work schedules had prevented them from hanging out as often as they wished, and having that extra day for the weekend would provide the needed time for bonding and comradery. The two lifelong friends had really missed each other's company and this was the perfect time to get together.

They were sharing old stories of happier times gone by as they drove around the city in CJ's newly purchased Chevrolet Monte Carlo.

CJ's memory flashed back to how they used to take long drives down to the shore in the summer months and short drives to New York City at other times.

He remembered that the very first car ever bought for him was a present for his 17th birthday - a vintage 1964 Chevrolet Impala and he has been driving Impalas ever since.

The two hadn't planned any agendas for this particular weekend; the idea was to be completely spontaneous and free-wheeling.

A beautiful aspect of this companionship was that they were quite opposite in many aspects, but fully complementary when important and sensitive issues mattered most. There was nothing that could interfere with their bonded brotherhood and they promised themselves many years ago to protect one another and always to watch each other's backs.

It was a gala weekend for these two friends. They enjoyed a drive to New York City and walked throughout lower Manhattan's Village where they visited a few popular cafes and small shops. On Saturday evening they made the journey to Madison Square Garden and watched the New York Knicks win an important NBA game.

The following day included a return trip to New York and a drive uptown to Harlem. They decided to enjoy a hot lunch at the famed Sylvia's restaurant and did a little shopping along 125th St. before returning home for a few games of spades with friends.

After playing spades the two sat down for a conversation about their favorite subject: women. It was during this conversation that CJ revealed the story about breaking his virginity as a birthday present.

"Wow," exclaimed O'Neil. "It's about time! I broke my virginity at age 14. Was it all that you expected it to be?"

"I'll say," CJ responded. "It was a thriller and much more. I don't know why it took me so long."

They had a hearty laugh, paused for a moment, and then said simultaneously:

"It was Cynthia!"

It was a good feeling for CJ that he could now laugh about her; it was a sign that he had finally overcome the misery and pain their breakup had caused him.

Suddenly CJ remembered there was a small bottle of champagne left in the fridge; it was a gift from Anna and Carnell. He retrieved the bottle and said, "This calls for a toast to celebrate women - the good, the bad, but not the ugly."

They both laughed while CJ poured the chilled wine, filling their glasses to the brim.

"This is to us, may our friendship last forever and a day."

The elders have a saying that the fortune that enters our lives comes to us in sets of three. CJ believed this had been true for him and was grateful for the three favors that had entered his life at this time. He silently thanked God for all of them.

The first was for being blessed to live long enough to witness becoming a man of legal age.

He counted as the second favor his realization of mental, emotional, and physical benefits of making love with a mature, experienced woman who helped him yield up his virginity.

The last was the opportunity to share a companionship that is non-judgmental and supportive, a lifelong and lasting friendship with O'Neil.

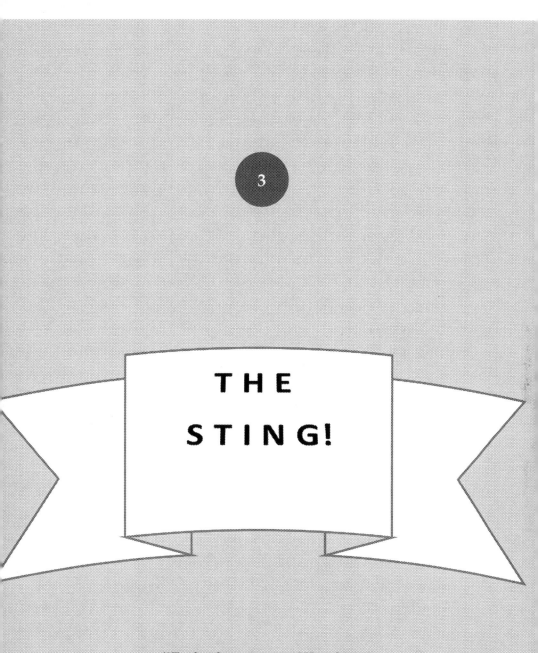

THE STING!

"Pain is not an illusion"

CHAPTER 9

The next life

There was a winter storm brewing, bringing emptiness and devastation to the Sinclairs' home.

Carnell hadn't been his normal energetic self since their returning from Cuba where he and Anna celebrated their silver anniversary. He struggled with loss of weight and vomiting, a lack of appetite, and feelings of listlessness. He exhausted most of his sick time at work and recently was calling out sick at least once a week.

He was a strong minded ex-solider man who didn't complain about most things and rarely had even a head cold. It was only Anna's persistent urging and love that finally compelled him to visit the doctors.

Anna and CJ were naturally worried and sought the opinions of several doctors; however, none was able to give any clarity as to what was happening to him.

One day during a scheduled visit at the Veterans Administration Hospital a blood specialist said his study of Carnell's blood samples could give no clues for a possible breakthrough in identifying the cause of his illness.

The doctor explained, "Within Carnell's blood supply something has been causing his immune cells to mutate or become damaged and they have begun to grow out of control, crowding out the healthy immune cells."

It all sounded Greek to the Sinclair family. They were only interested in one thing alone and they all simultaneously asked the doctor, "Can you fix it?"

The doctor answered, "We don't know at this time, but I will send my results abroad to a hospital in England to get further analysis. The only thing I can do at this time is to prescribe a stronger medication that will support his healthy blood cells."

The family took the doctor's statement as an offer of a small window of hope and continued to do the only thing they could: pray.

As a result of Carnell's illness and his inability to work steadily, the bills and household responsibilities for the family rested on the shoulders of CJ. Fortunately for him he was well prepared to handle the task, and very glad to do so.

During the previous three years CJ had received multiple promotions at work and several times had been named the employee of the month for his insightful contributions to the firm. He was highly respected by his boss and his colleagues and could look forward to more advancement opportunities. He lived a fairly simple life and was very prudent saving money and learning how to make investments that would allow his money to grow. Meanwhile Anna was inspired by her son's successes and found a part-time job she hoped would lessen the financial burdens.

The Sinclair family was determined to hang tough together and ride it out.

One day, while CJ was sitting at his desk at work and reading pamphlets about investments, his boss spoke to him about attending two seminars concerning income tax code changes and low-risk investment strategies. The two seminars would be held late in December, with all expenses paid in Washington, DC. His boss, the managing partner, said he had noticed his interest in these two matters and thought that he'd best represent the firm at the seminars.

CJ was honored and surprised that he was noticed by his boss and agreed to attend and learn all that he could. The seminars were being conducted at the year's end before the new tax season began, thus allowing anyone filing income tax returns to take advantage of new code provisions.

Only two weeks earlier, Sal Nardone had mentioned he would be referring CJ to more potential clients for preparing their annual tax returns. It was a part-time opportunity for CJ that would enable him to earn extra money while improving his skills.

The main reason for Sal's interest in CJ's tax skills was that he was looking for an edge to improve his tax position with regard to the property he owned within the Beehive district. New loopholes pertaining to commercial and business properties could profit him tremendously and he desired to take full advantage.

At the two-day seminar there were new people for CJ to meet and collaborate with on investment and tax strategies, both within the law and pushing its boundaries. It was his first time travelling to the nation's capital and in spite of the long hours he spent in meetings he was able to take in the sights and sounds of the capital mall and the White House. He made sure he brought back plenty of mementos for Anna and Carnell as neither of them had ever visited Washington, DC.

Upon his return to work he was asked to give a full presentation of all he had learned. He was prepared and delighted to do so and made a great impression on his boss and his colleagues.

The firm was very progressive and its principals made sure to keep abreast of any beneficial information that would increase their client base and help them stay ahead of the competition.

CJ could hardly wait for tax season to begin.

His first client was Sal Nardone, and he saved him thousands of dollars on his taxes. CJ also suggested that Sal give some thought to becoming an incorporated entity and placing his buildings under the umbrella of a corporation.

Sal was delighted with CJ's recommendations and to show his gratitude he encouraged many of his friends in government and his other associates to hire CJ to prepare their tax returns.

CJ was meticulous at finding obscure tax law provisions and using them to his clients' benefit. His biggest challenge that year was filing for the four largest and most lucrative businesses in the Beehive. The Sugar Cane, Cut and Curl, The Pony Express, and Heads Up" were all legal businesses up front and thereby eligible for deductions such as depreciation allowance. CJ was well aware of the illegal activities that took place behind the scenes which presented a potential problem, and he pledged to take care of all that in the very near future.

The Big Four all ended up paying far less than in previous years because of CJ and his expertise. Dee Dee and Artie of Dee Dee's Lounge offered him office space, which enabled him to prepare and file tax returns outside of the firm. They were truly grateful for the service he provided them and this was how they repaid him. Everyone was benefiting from his services and he soon became the talk of the town. He was protected and promoted by Mr. Sal, which gave him a respected position in all the neighborhoods, especially the Beehive district.

Some of the firm's more established clients continued to entrust their tax accounting to the firm, but many more personally went to CJ. In fact, his success and involvement in the community became the number one factor in increasing the client base at the firm. The managing partner of the firm understood what was happening; he knew he produced a "cash cow" and encouraged CJ to expand as he wished. The word on the streets about his skills became so widespread that for every tax return he completed there would be three new clients coming into the firm.

Tax season was very profitable for CJ as he filled out hundreds of forms for people in New Jersey and New York. At the conclusion of that tax season he deposited nearly $40,000 into his savings account. His huge success during tax season prompted recognition at the firm. He became the youngest member in the firm's history to become a partner, and within the shortest period of time

CJ had discovered a new passion within himself. He fully embraced the reality that he loved making money while beating the odds - he compared that to playing competitive chess - and he surely loved winning. The timing could not have been any better and the money he was earning definitely helped with family finances and Carnell's medical bills.

In spite of his professional achievements, CJ was not satisfied. He still yearned to do more by learning more about stocks, bonds, and anything else under the umbrella of investing.

One late afternoon while sitting at home meditating at his desk, CJ remembered a chance meeting with a financial advisor he was introduced to at the DC seminars. This gentleman impressed CJ so much that he swore he'd contact him in the near future for lunch and discuss some non-traditional investment options. He looked into his attaché case and located the gentleman's business card. It was a colorful depiction of large and small dollar signs with his name in bold green letters - Danny Mack, financial advisor and planner - known to his associates as D Mack.

Danny Mack was a medium-sized man but appeared larger due to his command of the English language, his highly fashionable wardrobe, and his Caribbean charm and good looks. He had grown quite wealthy over the years making assorted legal and illegal investments. He was known to travel throughout the world attending all kinds of seminars, conventions, and workshops pertaining to financial planning and asset growth.

He attended these events to learn rules and regulations and would then devise schemes to undercut or bend them for personal profit. His accumulated wealth included a substantial amount of international real estate. He also owned a Lear jet, high-yield bonds, and a portfolio of high-performing stocks.

During their initial meeting at the Washington, DC, seminar he was preparing to retire and was searching for someone with whom he could share his knowledge, insights, and strategies in hopes that the person he mentored would become as successful as he had been.

In time D Mack would become a valued asset for CJ, but CJ would only bend the rules and exploit the system for what he imagined to be a greater good rather than exclusively for personal profit. CJ did, however, admit to himself that he felt a relentless drive to become a millionaire by age 25.

Four months later, CJ initiated a call to D Mack. The two of them shared lunch. They talked for hours, exchanging investment ideas and insight into how the stock markets worked.

Mr. Sal suggested that CJ talk with D Mack and to learn what he could, while Sal did a background check to see if D Mack was legit. As expected the background check confirmed that D Mack was legitimate, which opened the door for more meetings.

They met often over the next several months as CJ became a willing student, learning all he could from his new mentor. It wasn't long before he was proficient in elaborate investing strategies and schemes.

It was CJ's brainstorm to broaden the scope of operations within the Beehive section and convert illegal profits into legal ones by investing them in legal businesses. He realized he would need Mr. Sal's influence and muscle for persuasion.

The weekly chess matches between Sal and CJ proved to be the optimum atmosphere for open conversations between the two. Sal was always intrigued by the progressive mindset of his young protégé and fully aware of his drive and hunger for advancement. As mentor, Sal would apply patience as the governing tool for any scenario that ushered from CJ's head.

"What's on your mind young man?"

"I've been doing a lot of thinking lately about investing and how it might serve all of us."

"When you say us, who in particular are you talking about?"

"I am referring to you, me, and some of the businesses in the Beehive district."

Mr. Sal paused to rear back into his chair, then politely said, "Please continue; I'm interested in what your vision would be."

CJ took a deep breath and then began to explain point by point a plan he thought would render the Big Four a robust return on their investments. He stated that the overall objective for the vice activities in the Beehive was to make a lot of money.

"I believe we can make much more and avoid the legal hassles and public scrutiny that accompanies those activities," CJ said. He began his presentation by reading to Mr. Sal the definition from Webster's dictionary of the word conglomerate:

A large corporation made up of many companies that operate in different and often entirely unrelated markets.

After giving some examples, he gathered up his research documents and delivered his pitch on his vision for the future.

The main theme was to form a conglomerate that would include the Big Four and perhaps other interested participants. He would teach them all how to invest their ill- gotten-gains, moving that money into investments that were likely to yield a high rate of return. In a short period of time their profits could be worth 40 times their initial investment, CJ told Sal.

He continued to assure Sal that the effort required for this was minimal compared to the expected results.

CJ further explained that he had identified a diverse group of possible domestic and international investments for which risks were low and the yields were expected to be very high.

He went on to say this would be no different from what J.D. Rockefeller, Andrew Carnegie and other multi-millionaires had done to develop and expand their empires while securing their fortunes for future generations.

He was convinced that this was the American ideal and the essence of what capitalism was based on. He also mentioned to Sal that, similar to the game of chess, all investing moves are calculated risks carefully thought out to ultimately lead to a successful conclusion; a victory.

The conversation continued for hours, delving into how it would work and what would be required to ensure its success. Sal was amazed at the amount of research and thoughtfulness that had gone into CJ's detailed and persuasive proposal. However, there was still a puzzling question that Sal couldn't ignore and so he asked, "I would like to know why you are discussing this with me."

"The reason is because you are the ideal leader of what and how anything takes place at the Beehive. The other reason is because I have always thought of those activities as a stain on the overall community and I would like to transform it into something far more legitimate and secure. Since the main objective is to make money, I came to you because if you accept this idea the others will follow."

Sal admired the confidence he observed in CJ and realized that this would take serious planning and strong financial backing. He was well aware that the services being provided through the Big Four were considered harmless vice that made money because the public showed a demand for it.

Over the years Sal Nardone had done quite well financially and lived comfortably as a result of the Beehive activities. The same vice enterprise provided him political and legal protections during his reign. He had become a kingpin of sorts; he was well respected and useful for those needing public support or assistance.

Sal was more powerful than both the mayor and the district attorney's office and he wasn't abusive or antagonizing with the use of that power. His friends and close acquaintances were very wealthy and reached into the governor's office and the U.S. Senate.

He recognized that change was good and he realized that he wouldn't remain in his position forever; in fact he was cautiously optimistic that CJ would be the obvious choice to evolve into that position through his mentorship. The two talked for a while longer and then set the board for their second game. At the conclusion of play Sal congratulated CJ for another spilt of their two games and then stated: "I have heard your proposal and I will give it serious consideration. Let me mull over the idea for a while and then I'll get back to you."

"Thank you," said CJ. "I appreciate you taking the time to listen and I will remain patient for your answers."

The two men stood up and shook hands as they did after each session of chess matches.

As Sal turn toward the alcove doorway he paused and then asked, "How is your father's health these days?"

"My dad isn't doing too well. He's in the intensive care ward and his prognosis is not good. I'm on my way there right now for a visit."

'I'm sending my prayers for him and Anna please give my regards."

"I will," said CJ, and, God willing, I'll see you next week."

It had been over a year since the doctors identified Carnell's unusual blood disease and even though there was hope, his condition continued to decline with no recovery in sight.

The emotional stress of Carnell's illness was a heavy burden for Anna, but she remained positive and optimistic for his recovery. The doctors were unable to develop a treatment plan that might arrest the progression of his illness, and finally they had to place him into hospice care.

As CJ arrived at the Veterans Hospital he was feeling somewhat apprehensive about this particular visit. His uneasiness may have been due to the staff doctor's prognosis the previous week that Carnell may not live another month. This was an emotional rollercoaster ride for Anna and CJ, but he knew he needed to stay strong and resolute for the good of the family.

Carnell was restfully asleep in a private room with monitoring equipment attached to his body. His skin had turned pale and his breathing was shallower than it had been during CJ's last visit of two days earlier. It was difficult seeing his father in this condition; he had always seen him as invincible and steady as a rock. The love they had shared was immeasurable and the thought of losing him was beginning to become a stark reality.

CJ stood at Carnell's bedside looking at him and remembering all the talks, good times, and advice he had received from his dad over these last 23 years. He was grateful for being raised by such a caring and dedicated father as Carnell and he always worked hard to make his dad proud. He smiled at his dad and for a brief moment he imagined him smiling back.

The ringing of alarm bells and flashing lights on one of the monitoring devices broke CJ's reverie. Instantly the doctors and aides rushed in. They ushered CJ out of the room while they attempted to remedy the situation.

Every second seemed like an hour as CJ waited nervously for them to open the door and beckon him back into the room.

When the door finally opened and CJ walked in, he could tell from their facial expressions that it wasn't good news. The intensive care doctor looked at CJ with a bowed head and said, "I'm sorry, son; your father has just passed away."

The sound of that statement didn't register immediately with CJ and he stood there, frozen in mind and in time. He gingerly walked toward his father's bedside.

CJ rubbed his fingers through Carnell's thinning hair and with tears forming in his eyes, he gently kissed him goodbye on the forehead. He silently offered one last prayer for his father and then talked with his doctors about gathering all of his personal effects and receiving the necessary death certificates. He thanked the doctors, nurses, and aides for the care given to his father and then he turned toward Carnell's body and saluted him goodbye.

"Thanks, Dad, I love you and I'll see you again on the other side."

The walk to the elevator seemed darker and longer than usual. Once outside, he simply couldn't remember where he had parked the car.

He somehow found the car, climbed into the driver's seat, and then let go of his emotions and began to cry. It was a special and private time he needed with God, himself, and the memory of his father.

The silence and time spent inside his car became a blanket of small comfort for CJ as he glanced up at the hospital room that held his father's body and then to the heavens as he exhaled a sigh of release.

The heavy task ahead of him was to regain a sense of resolve and be prepared to tell Anna the painful news.

The ride home was a slow and uncomfortable journey filled with remorse, as well as the strange comfort of being in the company of his father when he took his last breath. It was usually a half hour trip from the hospital to their home, but it took CJ more than an hour to finally arrive. He was wrestling with awkward feelings from that experience with death, the memory of which would remain with him for the balance of his life.

Anna was sitting on the front porch when CJ pulled into the driveway; she looked as though she knew something wasn't quite right. She looked into the watering eyes of her son and then without saying a word hugged him with all of her might. He whispered, "He's gone Mama; my dad has passed on."

CJ was careful not to use the word dead, thinking that would offer her some small comfort. They stood embracing for a long moment before going inside to sit in utter silence.

Anna walked to the fireplace mantel, picked up a picture of her and Carnell, and then sat down in his favorite chair. It was odd, CJ thought, because she never sat in his chair while he was alive, but she wanted to feel his presence one more time. As she held the picture tightly in her bosom, she began to cry. CJ sat at her feet on the carpeted floor and they continued to cry together.

The look on Anna's face was reflective of the accumulated stress that she had endured during the ordeal and time of Carnell's illness. It was a look unfamiliar to CJ - he had never seen his mother as anything but beautiful, composed, and strong. He wanted more than anything to remember her as she normally appeared. In all his years there wasn't a single time that he ever saw a sad or unpleasant look upon her youthful face.

He realized the impact of the current situation and he knew she would never be the same again.

The preparation for the funeral service was a four-day affair, and on the fifth day Carnell's body was laid to rest.

Carnell had left a hefty insurance policy for Anna, but CJ insisted he'd pay for everything himself. According to Carnell's final wishes, he preferred a simple, inexpensive funeral and had requested that Anna not spend all of the insurance money for the funeral as was customary in many families.

He was never an official member of any church nor was he ever baptized. However, Anna became a member of the Mount Calvary AME church and Carnell and CJ would attend from time to time.

Anna took the initiative to alert Carnell's remaining family members about his death and she invited and expected them all to attend. CJ made one phone call to Dee Dee's Lounge and spoke with Artie and Sal and from those two the word circulated throughout the city.

The response from the people toward this former war hero and beloved citizen was nothing short of amazing. The telephone rang day and night with people offering their condolences and desires to help. There were also visits to the Sinclair home by business owners, government officials, and even old army buddies. The flower arrangements and sympathy cards poured in by the dozens and members of Anna's Ladies Auxiliary brought cooked food and sat with her for prayers, comfort, and any needed assistance.

Mr. Sal arranged to have the local newspapers write a half page obituary about the life of their local war hero. The community support was overflowing with unparalleled love and appreciation. A parade of people from the Beehive area of town visited the Sinclair home with money-filled envelopes as an offering to offset the funeral cost. (It was a Southern tradition to donate money and food to the families of the deceased.) It was also very comforting for Anna and CJ to witness the love that the people showed for Carnell.

A compromise was struck between CJ and Anna concerning how the funeral would be conducted. Anna wanted the AME church to perform the services with a closed wooden casket and large picture of Carnell on top of it. Although he wasn't a member of the AME, she convinced the minister to offer final words a eulogy. CJ desired that Carnell's army friends perform the traditional 21-gun salute and present a glass- enclosed United States flag to Anna at the grave site.

The day of the funeral, the heavens opened up with smiles of warm sunshine and clear skies. The church was packed and the people came from far and wide to bid a solemn farewell to their beloved companion. Dee Dee's Lounge was closed in honor of Big C.

The funeral address wasn't long but its impact was moving and powerful. The minister talked about the supreme attributes and qualities of Carnell and his willingness to aid anyone in need. There were several emotional testimonials from friends, family, and government officials who talked about and highlighted the clam, spiritual nature of a wounded soldier who knew the value of sacrifice. In front of the church surrounding the coffin along with a picture of Carnell in full military dress was a magnificent display of floral arrangements in dazzling colors, a tribute befitting a dignitary.

That day, CJ heard too many remarks from people about how much he resembled his father in looks and demeanor. It was both embarrassing and complimentary. While the comments made him feel good, they also increased his feelings of missing and needing his father.

The ride to the cemetery overwhelmed CJ and he wept openly with his mother by his side. The last funeral he attended was for his grandfather, when he was only 5 years old and far too young to really understand what was happening. Now, as a grown man, he fully understood the final separation that death presents to the living.

As the grounds crew began to lower Carnell into the ground, loved ones placed red roses upon his coffin and blew kisses to him one last time. Anna and CJ thanked everyone for their support, quietly returned to the black limousine and headed home for the repast.

Later that day, many people came to visit and partake in a light meal and brief conversations before offering their final condolences and departing.

It was a full week and even fuller day for Anna and CJ; they were exhausted and only wanted to relax and sleep. There were shared compliments between them as they reviewed how the funeral proceeded and ended. Anna had the last word by simply saying, "Your father would have been so proud of you today. Thank you, son. I love you."

Eerie quiet that seemed to engulf their house as the day was ending was the spirit of Carnell coming to check on his loved ones.

Carnell's heavy spirit came to visit that night and it loomed over Anna and Charles. This spirit had watched them drift off to sleep with CJ sprawled on the couch and Anna slumped down into Carnell's chair. The silence and serenity of this scene was suddenly interrupted by a loud voice that echoed throughout the living room:

"I see you, and soon you will see me. I am done with this life and I'll see you in the next."

Anna and CJ sat up, looked at one another, and said,

"Did you hear that?"

"Yes, son, I heard it. That was Big C saying goodnight."

CHAPTER 10

The b. h. conglomerate

It had been two weeks since the burial ceremonies for Carnell had taken place. The remaining family - Anna and CJ - were trying to adjust from his being absent from home but at the hospital to never seeing, touching, or talking to him again - two very different realities.

The absence of Carnell would remain a test for both of them as they put back the torn pieces of their lives and began to move forward again.

The memories of Carnell and all of his lessons concerning life and love would remain with them forever.

Whenever the need arises for insight arises they will be able to tap into those memory banks and Carnell will respond. They will remain forever connected by way of pictures in the scrap book, a favorite song of his, or perhaps by lounging in his favorite chair.

Although death is final on this earthly plain, it is never absolute in our spirits, minds, and emotions during the time that remains for those still living.

It was a daily struggle with Anna as she fought hard to maintain her composure every time she stepped into a room, or looked at a picture, or smelled a scent from his clothes still hanging in their closets. She knew that she would have to re-arrange many things in the house to release some of the reminders, and that it would take some time.

Adapting to the new reality was different for CJ, not because his memory was less but because he plunged himself deeper into his work. Whenever he was out or about he had to respond to his father's associates reminding him of how much he resembled Big C. And then there were the medical bills and remaining responsibilities at home that needed his attention. He often thought all of this might be better handled if he only had a love in his life to share his burden.

Despite the distractions of their daily routines, he and Anna held their wits about them and remained positive to simply forge ahead with each passing day.

One early Sunday afternoon toward the end of May when Anna had returned from church and was preparing one of her sumptuous meals, the doorbell rang and there, standing on the front porch, were two people she didn't recognize.

"CJ, can you answer the door; I'm in the kitchen."

"Yes, Mom, I'll get it right away."

Standing at the doorway was a distinguished looking gentleman and a beautiful younger lady smiling and standing by his side.

Anna put aside her apron and rushed to the door to see who it was and what they wanted.

"Good afternoon, Ma'am," the man said. "Please allow me to introduce myself.

My name is Stanley Gillman, but most of my friends prefer to call me Stan. Your late husband and I were good friends in the service together. This young lady is Shelly Gillman. She is my daughter and we brought this token gift as condolence."

"It's nice to meet you both, won't you please come in and have a seat."

"Thank you," said Stan. "I'm sorry that we are late, I received the news about Carnell but we were in Europe on business and this is the earliest I could get here. I don't want to take up much of your time, but I need to explain to you my relationship with Carnell and exactly why I am here."

`"I appreciate your visit. I am Anna and this is our son, Charles; most people call him CJ. Please let me take your hat and sweater while you make yourselves comfortable. I just made some fresh coffee. May I offer any of you a cup?"

"I'll take a cup," said Stan. "The flight back to the states was long and tiring. We stopped at Shelly's place in New York City to change clothes and then we wanted to come right over as soon as possible. I didn't have the phone number, so please forgive us for the intrusion."

"No, please don't apologize. I'd love to talk with anyone who knew of my husband and his ties to the military."

"Excuse me for interrupting you, Anna, but I didn't just know him; your husband saved my life on two different occasions."

Anna was surprised, because Carnell never bragged or talked much about his military service or the medals he received for valor. She was intrigued and braced herself for the story to unfold. Anna always felt honored by her husband's military service, and she looked upon him as though he were 10 feet tall.

In that moment she recalled the many outings they attended and the respect shown to her from men and women alike. She attributed that respect to Carnell's demeanor, self-respect, and the way he carried himself at all times.

She and CJ sized up their guests while Stan talked.

Stanley was about 6 feet tall. He was very handsome, impeccably dressed, and well-groomed from head to toe. His daughter was strikingly beautiful, but much shorter, and she too was fashionably dressed and groomed as though she were a fashion model or a Hollywood actress. CJ politely shook both their hands and took his hat and her sweater before escorting them to sit down on the leather sofa. Shelly handed him the sweet dish she had prepared for them and as he received it their eyes locked into one another's and smiles appeared upon both their faces.

"Hi, I'm CJ. It's so nice to meet you."

"Yes, it is CJ, and I'm sure the pleasure is mine."

He sat next to her on the sofa, waiting for Stan to begin the story of his father's rescues. Oddly enough their eyes and smiles kept meeting and CJ relaxed as though he had known her from another time in his life.

Shelly must have felt the same way, because she reached for his hand and clenched it as her father shared stories of Carnell's valor. The connection between them was electric.

Stan went on to tell a detailed and emotional tale of how Carnell dragged him from a grenade attack his unit had suffered at the hands of enemy troops in Italy. It was pure courage. Stanley and many of his men lay wounded and dying as enemy troops were closing in. Carnell drove his jeep into the area of the wounded mass of men, Stan recounted, pulling three men into the jeep and then driving away to safety. Once they were within a safer area he used his medical kit to bandage the wounded and stop the bleeding.

"I would have lost my leg completely, or possibly died, if he hadn't rescued us in the timely fashion that he did. I was his unit commander during that time and he was part of the supply line that delivered our ammunition. He wasn't responsible for our aid but he reacted quickly and decisively, and his heroic actions saved lives. It was I who recommended that he receive a medal for exhibiting bravery above and beyond the call of duty.

"The second time, a time in France when we were again under attack from German troops, I was shot in the arm and couldn't retrieve my gun. Carnell came to me and picked up my machine gun and began firing back to repel the enemy forces. This act enabled us to retreat to higher ground and a better position. We won that fierce battle and proceeded to captured 45 German soldiers.

"I say without a doubt that if it wasn't for the quick reaction of Carnell and his courage to fire back we may have all been captured by the Germans."

Stan paused for a moment, took a sip of his coffee, and then slowly said, "I am the only living survivor of the three that he saved, and I need to settle this debt.

"After the war ended I repeatedly tried to thank and repay him somehow, but because of his pride he would never accept anything from me; he always said he was just trying to be a good soldier.

"My fortunes changed when I came back into the states and I invested into the textile industry. I own several textile mills in North Carolina, Peru, India, and Pakistan and a leather tannery in Texas. I am a major fabric supplier for the top fashion industries throughout the world. After many years of hard work and a little luck I have evolved to become a successful businessman with a net worth commensurate to the size of my holdings.

"My daughter Shelly is a leading fashion and jewelry consultant and also my number one business partner. I remained a resident of Dallas, Texas, although I travel a lot with Shelly these days. My daughter decided to reside in New York City because of the concentration of fashion and jewelry businesses in Manhattan, but my heart lives in Texas."

Stan looked up at Anna and CJ, took a breath, and continued.

"I am here to offer my heartfelt condolences and to finally repay my debt.

"I had my accountant do some checking and I know that this house is not yet paid off and that you are paying off the medical bills that Carnell accrued. My offer to you both is to pay off all those debts and allow you to become debt free.

"Please allow me this one request; it's the least I can do before I leave this world."

Anna and CJ were sitting in shock and Shelly was tearing up after hearing the story for the first time. CJ softly patted her hand as a small gesture of support, and then offered her a handkerchief from his pocket, remembering what his father had taught him: "Always carry a handkerchief - you'll never know when a women will need it."

When Shelly turned to thank him, CJ had his first opportunity to really assess her beauty and maturity.

Her skin was flawless and her subtle makeup was professionally applied with soft touches. Her eyes were olive green and her blonde hair sparkled against her golden tanned skin. She was a little shorter than CJ and her shapely legs that were crossed giving her a youthful appearance that belied her age.

He desperately tried to be polite and not stare, but her wide and infectious smile made that seem impossible. CJ wasn't sure of the signals she was sending - maybe she was showing her gracefulness or offering polite condolences - but whatever it was, he clearly wanted to know more about her and would carefully wait for the opportunity to present itself.

Anna suddenly arose from the sofa and returned with Carnell's frayed old army scrapbook. She had seen it dozens of times, but never made the connection to Stan until now. She remembered that Carnell was a member of a segregated unit and yet she recalled a picture of a few white men standing among them. She handed the book to Stan and as he thumbed through it he paused, smiled, and then pointed to himself in a black and white picture.

"That's me standing right behind Carnell," he said. "We had just arrived in Italy."

Shelly and CJ stood up to observe the picture and confirm that it was indeed him. The atmosphere in the living room quickly changed from the gloom of wartime memories to one of joy as they smiled at the old photo.

Stan announced that he and Shelly needed to get back to New York;

he then urged Anna and CJ to ponder his offer in the next few days and then contact Shelly with an answer.

They agreed to respond and then casually walked their surprise guests toward the door. Shelly gave her phone number to CJ before leaving the Sinclair home. With a smile she insisted that he call her sooner rather than later. The four of them hugged and thanked one another.

Anna and CJ stood on the front porch, watching and waving as Shelly and Stan drove away in a shiny, new, red Cadillac convertible.

That evening, Anna and CJ talked, agreeing their visitors were a sign from God and Carnell, who were watching over them. By accepting Stan's offer, they could eliminate their debts to and bring peace of mind into their lives.

After preparing herself for bed that night, Anna fell upon her knees and prayed to Almighty God, thanking Him for their blessings. She wiped away the flowing tears from her eyes before falling off to a gentle sleep.

CJ remained awake a little longer. He was recalling the tales of heroic deeds his father had performed and feeling good about the man they called Big C. He also had many pleasurable thoughts of Shelly roaming about in his head; he imagined that if he were an artist how easy it would be to sketch a picture of her from recent memory. He thought about calling her to satisfy his desire of getting to know her better. The thought had barely cleared his mind when the telephone rang. It was Shelly's soft voice on the phone.

"I'm just calling to thank you again for your family's hospitality, and I was wondering if you would accept an invite for a luncheon date for you and me."

CJ couldn't believe his ears and he didn't want to seem too anxious; he paused for a brief moment, and then happily answered with a resounding yes. The phone call continued for another 25 minutes as the two exchanged small pleasantries before bidding each other a fond goodnight.

It was then that CJ also fell upon his knees, thanking Almighty God for the visit and the phone call, and, finally, for a possible new chapter opening in his life.

In two days, CJ made the call to Shelly to inform her of their decision to accept the generous offer from Stanley. She told him that her father had returned to Texas, but she would ensure that within a few days the situation would be resolved.

Since he was feeling better due to Shelly Gillman entering his life, CJ felt the need for a good game of chess with Sal Nardone. He also wanted to talk with Sal about something that was uppermost in his mind: the proposal to form a conglomerate with the Big Four. CJ was eager to hear what Sal's considered opinion would be.

After playing three games at Dee Dee's Lounge later that week, they took a break to discuss the proposed business venture.

Sal thought the proposal was brilliant and he believed that he could convince the Big Four to accept the idea as well. He conveyed to CJ that he needed two weeks to set up a meeting and then he wanted him to give his presentation to the group. It was a challenge that CJ would be ready for. The extensive research and preparation he had done would inform his delivery of a well-conceived plan.

The motivation behind this novel idea was a promise he made to himself that he would be a millionaire by the age of 25. He had planned it in the same manner as a well-designed chess strategy and he was thoroughly convinced he would be victorious in just two years.

There would be plenty of time before the big meeting and CJ was definitely ready for some down time of relaxation and enjoyment - and he looked forward to the upcoming luncheon with Shelly.

The luncheon with Shelly had proved to be much more valuable than he ever imagined. She had made a 1 p.m. reservation for two at one of New York City's most iconic restaurants, Tavern on the Green. The lavish style and setting of this fine restaurant is world renowned and attracts elite patrons.

Shelly had arranged this luncheon because she needed to make a closer evaluation of CJ outside the comfort of home and his mother. She had sensed something unique, mysterious, and sensual about CJ and she was very attracted to him from first sight. It was the feminine instincts that intrigued her and propelled her to find out more about him. She always relied on and followed those instincts.

It was a routine practice of CJ to arrive anywhere earlier than scheduled; he did this so that he could survey the environment, send a signal concerning his promptness, and demonstrate that he was serious about time. He mentioned to the waiter that he was awaiting the arrival of his guest and then positioned himself for a wide-angle view of all who entered.

Shelly arrived seven minutes ahead of schedule. When she crossed the threshold CJ watched with admiration and approval.

The measured strides she'd taken toward him filled him with delight and he knew immediately that this was a woman of confidence and sensuality. She was immaculately clad in beige, white, and yellows with matching shoes and a small, artistic arrangement of diamonds and pearls that delicately encircled her wrist and slim neckline. A small yellow daisy was smartly tucked into what appeared to be a freshly finished hair design. She smiled and extended her dainty hand to him and then said with a Texas drawl, "Well, how are you CJ? Have you been waiting long? Are you very hungry or would you like a cocktail first?"

CJ gently accepted her hand, softly kissing the back of it while inhaling the sweet smells of skin and perfume that emanated from it. He complimented her on the spring - like colors she was wearing and reinforced his observations with, "you look stunningly gorgeous."

Shelly would probably intimidate the average man with her self-assured manner of being, but CJ was intrigued with what he had noticed thus far.

"I haven't been here long, but let's get seated first, and then we can decide."

Shelly nodded at the waiter that they were ready to be seated. The two of them were then escorted to a quiet corner table adjacent to a floor-length window that looked out over the garden of the grand, Gothic style landmark restaurant.

This was the first visit for CJ, and he was immensely impressed with the interior decor and the splendid service. It was obvious that Shelly had been there before, because the waiters knew her by name.

Cocktails, the meal, and the desserts were sublime, as was their wide-ranging conversation that touched on likes and dislikes, friends and family, career paths, and the future.

Shelly was a shrewd conversationalist, diving into subjects that comforted CJ and opened him up beyond his normal shyness. He learned that she was three years his senior, well-traveled, enjoyed poetry and - more importantly - that she dabbled in a good chess game from time to time.

Shelly was living alone in a three-bedroom condominium on the upper east side of Manhattan and she invited CJ to join her in a friendly game at his leisure. Although this was their first chance to meet and talk freely, there wasn't anything that he didn't totally admire about her.

After their meal and stimulating conversations they strolled leisurely along the promenade, hand in hand while enjoying the fresh scents of blossoming flowers in the mist of springtime. It was still early afternoon and the full enjoyment of each other's company had made it seem as though time was being suspended especially for them. The conversations continued to easily flow, and, because Shelly had a unique sense of humor, they shared much spontaneous laughter and joy.

As they turned a corner on the path, CJ abruptly stopped, turned to Shelly, and asked, "Are you seeing anyone special these days?"

Shelly was somewhat surprised by the question, but secretly she was anticipating it and felt relieved that he finally ask her. As she turned and stepped closer training her soft, beautiful, green eyes on his face she replied, "No. I am not seeing or interested in anyone these days, except you!"

She went on to explain that she hadn't dated in more than nine months. The man she previously had been seeing now resided in Europe and was responsible for swindling her out of many thousands of dollars of assets.

"I am only interested in you and I was extremely attracted to you the very first time I laid eyes on you. I hoped this luncheon could remove any obstacles that might exist between us and that I could get to know you better."

CJ gave a long sigh of relief and then said to her, "Thank you for your honesty. I have been waiting for someone like you for more than two years, finally you have arrived."

He was looking down at her eyes and at that tender moment, he felt her expressing nothing but sincerity. She leaned much closer, looking up at him as their lips openly met with full intensity and passion.

They continued to talk while trading joyful looks at one another and walking into the sunlight of an early love. When they parted that day, they reinforced the promise to build upon what had begun and make it stronger going forward.

The time he had shared with Shelly inspired CJ. He became more motivated and he energetically prepared for the Big Four presentation.

Sal had spoken with the four owners and everyone was in agreement that the presentation would take place in a meeting room at the Sugar Cane. The Big Four owners weren't as enthusiastic as Sal about the idea of a change in direction for their profits; however they viewed any prospect for making money as worthy of their attention.

Sal was able to see the bigger picture. He knew that sooner or later their means of doing business wouldn't be sustainable, and in the end they would all lose or be incarcerated.

He was also aware the four owners could be wary of someone as young and uninvolved as CJ giving them advice about their businesses. It was their past histories with Sal that piqued their interest in the first place and brought them to the table to listen.

Sal was a forward thinker and believed in his young protégé; he believed he was on to something bigger than what they had achieved, and he was willing to invest time and money in this new plan. After all, it was Sal who owned the many politicians and police who often looked the other way. Also it was Sal who invested money for the startup of their businesses. He saw this as an opportunity for the future to take advantage of it now. If they didn't do it soon, he reasoned, someone else would.

The morning of the scheduled presentation, CJ was feeling supremely confident and believed he was doing the right thing. He knew that if he did this correctly the negative history of the Beehive would fade into obscurity.

He offered a prayer for his success before proceeding to the Sugar Cane lounge.

The meeting began with a simple but through explanation of the word conglomerate, a word that not all the local business owners were familiar with. CJ explained the word by using the human hand as a metaphor. "The human hand has five fingers, but each finger can move independently of the others; however when they curl together to form a clenched fist, they can deliver a powerful strike.

In other words, he said, a conglomerate is a corporation made up of several smaller, independently run companies, which may operate across several sectors and industries.

That analogy seemed to hold their attention and he continued by explaining that the Big Four are operating as individuals and thereby competing against each other; but if they were incorporated as one, then they would be able to expand, compete at a worldwide level, and increase their profits by volumes.

During the presentation CJ looked like a college professor. He had developed charts, graphs, and assorted clippings from newspapers and magazines to demonstrate how the corporate economy works. His research had shown substantial proof of the growth and record profits it produced.

He shared with his select audience a list of some popular forms of investing, directing their attention to peer-to-peer lending and the stocks of corporations that financial experts had identified as having exceptional growth potential.

He further explained that the art of investing profits for the purpose of money laundering wasn't a criminal offense at the time, but would likely become one in the future. Whenever public officials turn their attention to how money laundering works to deprive government of tax revenue, the practice will become criminalized, CJ forecast.

"The time to act was now," he emphasized, adding that he would prove and guarantee their profits would surpass their initial investment by 100 percent in the first year alone.

"Investment opportunities are wide open," CJ said in closing. "I will leave you with a list of several avenues you may wish to explore: real estate and development, food franchises, pharmaceutical research and development, professional sports marketing, and robotics."

After two hours of speaking and fielding questions, he finally saw their heads begin to nod and smiles to appear on their previously blank faces. Sal was beaming with pride in the vision his protégé had thoroughly explained and CJ knew that he could pull it off and maintain Sal's reputation for finding a niche in which to succeed. Everyone seemed pleased about the presentation and eager to get the project started.

Sal assured them that he would work out, with CJ's advice, targeted industries in which to invest and the initial cost to each participant, and then get back to them within two weeks. CJ had already anticipated their concerns and had worked out the numbers and target markets; but he agreed with Sal to sit and work it all out.

The only aspect that he hadn't addressed was contacting a good corporate lawyer to prepare the paperwork for incorporating b.h. Inc. He thought perhaps Shelly could be helpful finding a suitable attorney.

After all, she had incorporated her own highly successful business and partnered with her father in his enterprises. CJ felt he could trust her and he was confident she would respond in a positive, helpful manner.

He was mentally exhausted from the session with the Big Four but was feeling good about how it went. All he wanted to do now was spend some quality time with Shelly and be in the comfort of her loving embrace.

He telephoned her as soon as he arrived home and waited patiently to hear that slight, lingering drawl when she answered the phone. "Hello CJ; I've been awaiting your call. I miss you and can hardly wait to see you again."

'I miss you too baby; and if you're not too busy tomorrow perhaps we can visit the Metropolitan Museum and have lunch."

"It will be my pleasure, my dear," she replied. "And if you're up for it afterwards you can join me at my place for a friendly game of chess."

After his phone conversation with Shelly he took a long, hot shower and climbed into bed. As he pulled the bed sheets over his freshly cleaned body he kept recycling that passionate word that echoed over and over in his head - S-h-e-l-l-y.

CHAPTER 11

Busted

In the game of chess there is one primary rule - to think three or more moves ahead and also anticipate counter moves. And the masters require a process of planning seven to ten moves ahead.

Thinking ahead was the rule CJ applied as a guiding life principle, whether he was working at the firm or navigating his car through difficult traffic. This application earned him various kinds of victories far beyond the chess boards. The thought of failing at most things tried in his life would hardly cross his mind. Success, however, never tarnished CJ or caused him to become arrogant or ungrateful; in fact it magnified his humility.

As a result of his habit of planning ahead, the thought of failing at things he tried would hardly have crossed his mind. He was confident that the b.h. conglomerate idea depended on the dedication to create and maintain the corporate model he had recommended.

CJ wasn't naïve about the criminal behavior of the Big Four or what they were capable of doing. His concentration, however, would remain focused on planning and following through, based on the information he obtained through research.

The plan for b.h. Inc. was several years in the making and CJ pledged that it wouldn't be derailed by malice, jealousy, or greed. His was depending on his longtime relationship with Sal Nardone to ensure that didn't happen.

CJ's habit of being a prolific reader enabled him to anticipate Sal's questions concerning where and why to invest. His research afforded him insight into what types of products, inventions, and technology would be in the public demand for the near future.

The industries he would target for large capital investments from b.h.

Inc. included electronics, robotics, food processing, real estate development, pharmaceuticals, and professional sports paraphernalia.

He further envisioned making contributions to political campaigns and lobbying on behalf of b.h. Inc. interests.

Meanwhile, his desire to spend more time with Shelly was prominent in his mind. He needed to explain to her the scope of his plan and the benefits he hoped it would bring.

Shelly lived in a very comfortable three-bedroom condominium located at 227 East 66th Street in New York City on the 5th floor. Her home was lavishly decorated with the highest quality French-designed furnishings. Her interiors were delicately balanced with softly accented colors, expensive artwork, and colorful wall murals. A large lead crystal chandelier hung from the raised ceiling of her dining room. Imported marble, plush wall-to-wall carpets and imported hardwoods covered her floors.

As beautiful as all of this was, it paled in contrast to the Texas mansion where she once resided. By most comparisons she lived like a queen. In spite of her life of privilege, the beautiful and balanced grace of Shelly's personality rarely showed any signs of arrogance.

Shelly could be a very sociable being, but she preferred not to have many friends in New York City outside of the two fashion stores and one jewelry boutique that she owned. Shelly had never married, nor did she have any children; she was comfortable in her role as a loner until she met and began a love relationship with CJ.

Her neighborhood was home to a diverse cross-section of nationalities, religions, races, and economic status, from young professionals to retirees. It was a serene and secure residential area with gift shops, restaurants, and recreational facilities scattered about. Residents enjoyed their lifestyle in a well-designed and well-lit tree lined neighborhood. It was a place where dog walking and light exercising were daily routines and It was common for people to take leisurely strolls at various times during the night without hesitation or fear of criminal activities.

Shelly's was a close-knit neighborhood where everyone knew each other and respected one another's privacy while being mindful of the security of the entire community. Whenever CJ visited Shelly he felt as though he was transported into a different and a new society - free from judgement and bigotry; a society that embraces our naturalness to love and identify with our common humanity.

Despite the cultural and racial differences between them, CJ and Shelly always felt they were in a joyful haven whenever they shared one another's company in her East Side community.

CJ's Sundays had previously been reserved for spending time at home with Anna, but now CJ traveled to New York to be with Shelly. One Sunday afternoon when he arrived, Shelly had a surprise waiting for him. It was an imported marble chess set and table complete with a lounge chair and ottoman. They would play some very competitive chess games sitting there and it would be the first time for CJ to be challenged by a female.

Shelly mentioned that the lounge chair was his to relax or read in and that no one else was to sit in it. That chair reminded CJ of the one his father once sat in and how it was preserved only for him. He thanked her for the lovely gift and said it made him feel very special and loved. It was his little corner of the world whenever he was there, and he was thankful that Shelly had created it for him.

The two of them were spending a lot of quality time together and enjoying all the cultural and social events that New York City had to offer. Sometimes it would only be the two of them and at other times they'd go on double dates with O'Neil and his often- changing girlfriends. CJ was being exposed to a new and exciting world that included cultural happenings such as operas at the Metropolitan, hot-ticket Broadway shows, symphonies, poetry readings, sporting events, and multi-cultural celebrations held in Central Park.

He was embracing the New York lifestyle and enjoying every minute of it. Whenever they traveled people complemented them as the loving couple they appeared to be - and CJ's friends had crowned her with a nick name of Eggshell because of her flawless, lightly tanned skin.

One of Shelly's attributes was being an open-minded person free of judgements or reservations. CJ had discovered this and felt comfortable discussing any and all things with her. He appreciated receiving varied suggestions, based on her experiences and intelligence. In the jargon of chess, he had been check mated by the queen.

On a rainy and calm Sunday afternoon when they had just completed an intense chess match, CJ decided to speak with Shelly concerning his intentions for the b.h. conglomerate. He began explaining that his desire was to change the atmosphere of vice, corruption, and illegal activities that had plagued his city for a period of more than 35 five years. He told her he believed that since money was the common denominator in the Beehive district, he could expand the business owners' profit margins by a series of smart investments and thereby change the dynamics of the district.

Shelly was immensely impressed with his concern for the Beehive neighborhood. She thought CJ's idea for transforming the district's profits from backroom vice into legitimate and profitable investments was novel, and she and she told him she believed it could work. She also pledged to give him any support needed to make it a success.

Shelly was fully invested in the stock market and had made much money from her investments. She was also willing to give CJ suggestions about stocks that would be the best fit for the b.h. investors while expanding her own investment opportunities. She surprised CJ with a suggestion for them to become silent partners for b.h. Inc. without the principals' knowledge.

Her suggestion was a brilliant defensive chess move designed to protect CJ from the criminal element surrounding the Big Four. She was thinking ahead that one day they might turn against him in spite of the money he had made for them. She also informed him that over the years of partnership in her father's textile businesses they had gathered a cache of brilliant attorneys who waited at the ready if ever needed.

Three weeks had passed since the presentation from CJ to the Big Four and he was waiting patiently to hear from Sal while anticipating getting started. When they finally met, Sal apologized to CJ for the delay and said he had done some research on his own. The successful investors that he trusted had confirmed that CJ was on to something big and the proposal was primed for success.

Sal also said that he had some good news and bad news to report. The good news was that everyone was on board to begin the paperwork to incorporate the conglomerate. The bad news was he had received some reliable information from two cops on his payroll. They reported that a new and ambitious district attorney was being appointed, and he had political designs to shut down the Beehive.

His sources further explained this new district attorney was aggressively starting an investigation that could lead to several subpoenas or worse. Sal said he realized the information from his two cronies simply meant that the time was ripe and they needed to get going to avoid the political pressure that was sure to come. CJ agreed and then suggested how much startup capital would be needed.

The figure that CJ had in mind was for each member of the Big Four to make the initial investment of $100,000. He and Sal would have to put up the remaining amount for a total of $5 million. Each member would receive 20 percent of the net profits and CJ would get two percent from each of them.

They selected a corporate attorney recommended by Shelly with offices in midtown Manhattan, where Sal and the Big Four signed the paperwork to establish b.h. Inc.

CJ's calculations projected a very good return in a relatively short period of time. He recommended three companies or groups of companies that had the best potential for immediate success from the Big Four's initial investment.

The first was a robotics engineering company located in Germany. Industry experts believed their designs for robotic arms would revolutionize the automobile industry - and manufacturing worldwide - allowing those industries to mass produce with greater efficiency, thus creating a higher volume of profits.

The second initial investment would be in a Japanese electronics firm that was designing electrical components that would revolutionize the use of communication methods, telephone devices, surveillance, and the recording industry.

The third would be global textiles, dominated by corporations in the US, Britain and Malaysia. These companies were experimenting with techniques for producing clothing, furniture, construction materials, and a variety of new industrial fabrics using polymers and advanced technology.

The three investment opportunities CJ had identified were consistently highlighted in major financial periodicals worldwide. Over time, the predictions of their standout performance were right and those three industries transformed the way in which we live.

During the first six months of their stock market investing, everyone was learning and paying close attention to the ebb and flow of the market. It was a steep yet valuable learning curve that taught and encouraged them to explore and learn. In the first two years, growth exceeded all projections and netted them a total $6 million. The Big Four's conglomerate investing plan was working and everyone was ecstatic about the results.

A celebration, ignited by the pouring of vintage champagne, was held at Dee Dee's Lounge. Shelly was invited. She danced exclusively with CJ.

Not surprisingly Shelly was also the source and center of everyone's conversation and attention; it was obvious she belonged to CJ and some jealous patrons wanted to know who she was and where she'd come from. It wasn't long before CJ felt compelled to respond to the stares, winks, and chatter. He casually grabbed the microphone and Shelly's hand at the same time and then asked the musicians to lower the volume for a minute. He introduced her proudly as his loving girlfriend and loyal companion.

After hearing the passion of his words, the entire crowd at Dee Dee's erupted in cat-calls, whistles, and applause. Shelly was embarrassed by the introduction but she didn't hesitate to plant a long and passionate kiss in front of everyone. She was the object of attention, not just because It she was white, but because she was also beautiful, stylish, and confident. She displayed a lot of soul, and she could dance!

The joy of celebrating lasted far into the night before CJ and Shelly retired to her home for a blissful and even longer night of passionate lovemaking. Exhilarated but exhausted, the two lovers finally collapsed into a deep slumber that lasted late into Sunday morning.

The following Monday the Big Four met to consider the next moves for their now successful conglomerate. Not everyone was happy for their success and the seeds of jealousy were being planted by those in the Beehive district who weren't invited to become members of the conglomerate.

After dividing the profits and setting aside a percentage for taxes, CJ suggested that they reinvest 25 percent of the net profits and begin focusing on greater diversification.

Anticipating that the district attorney would be coming after them soon, the Big Four decided to select projects that would legitimize their current businesses and protect them from any possible criminal hassles that might occur. CJ and Shelly began the necessary research into opportunities and he outlined for the conglomerate principals a menu of several possibilities:

remodeling and expanding their existing legitimate businesses, building homes or apartments, becoming financially active in political campaigns to ensure their protection, purchasing land for business development, buying gold, putting some money into building and operating new hotels, or investing in farming, ranching, and food packaging.

The list was aggressive, with big projects proposed, but they all thought it was doable and they were very motivated to tackle the challenge. Timing and planning would be the key to success in this next phase of investing. The two projects that deemed most viable - and most feasible in the near term - were remodeling and expanding their individual businesses, and real-estate developing.

CJ requested a break of a few weeks before undertaking the second phase of diversification.

The purchasing of new cars, furnishings, jewelry, and fine clothing was the order of the day for most of the newly prosperous investors, but not for CJ. His motif was to be careful, disciplined, and not to draw any new attention to himself. He purchased some new furniture for Anna, bought her a car, and taught her how to drive, hoping she would seek a level of independence and not solely rely on him.

Anna had recently discovered her younger sister was living and barley surviving in New York City. Since they were both alone, she invited her to come and live with her in New Jersey, where she could commute to work via the N J Transit. It was a perfect plan that worked for them and it gave CJ more time for work and research.

CJ managed to keep a low profile and also seriously enjoy the moments of high life whenever spending time with his beloved Shelly. He kept a small amount of his earnings from his accounting job in the bank and rarely signed his name to any papers pertaining to b.h Inc. activities. The money he earned from the conglomerate was hidden in a vault in the crawl space of his home. He learned of this idea from Shelly, who had a vault designed and built behind the wall of her fireplace in her New York home.

CJ shared many of his ambitious ideas with Shelly. One idea was to buy land in the Pocono Mountains of Pennsylvania after accruing his second million dollars. It was his plan for them to own it together and build a few sophisticated resorts for tourists. It would remain a source for continued investing for maintenance and up-keep, well into the future.

The other idea was to open a chain of beauty and massage spas from east coast to the west. The final project he wanted to do himself was to build an addition to the AME church where Anna was a member. He was determined to get these projects done within the next three years, with Shelly by his side as a silent partner.

Sal proposed starting some construction projects as the first target of their diversification plan. He decided to buy up dilapidated properties that were eyesores in the Beehive district and build modest apartment buildings and a three-star hotel. The idea was to transform the physical look of the district and possibly attract other investors who would purchase the land from the b.h. conglomerate. There was also the prospect of creating jobs for the community and providing a better place to live.

Sal thought the time was appropriate for them to give financial support to any and all political candidates at local and state levels. They would come in handy and provide a level of protection while advocating for b.h. Inc. in the event the Big Four were ever investigated.

The second round of investments proved to be an even bigger success than the first. The Big Four had come up with all kinds of creative means of diversifying and their earnings were pouring in far beyond their expected projections. Each member of the conglomerate found a niche they were comfortable with and this allowed them to expand their original businesses, making even more money.

Sal owned two construction companies and a successful real estate firm that were building major projects throughout the tristate area. He also purchased 100 acres of prime land in suburban and rural New Jersey townships, with plans to develop business centers, luxury homes, and space for professional offices.

The owner of the Sugar Cane had established several recording studios in different parts of the country for new jazz artists, and a number of them had produced platinum selling recordings. He also opened jazz clubs in New York, Chicago, London, San Francisco, and New Orleans, all of which featured the top recording jazz artists in the business.

The Heads Up owner diversified his earnings into the pornography with top rated magazines and videos for adult audiences worldwide. He developed adult film boutique shops and video recording studios for pornography throughout California and New York. He employed male and female models from Europe, South America, and the United States. The most successful aspect of his business was an escort service, which he expanded into more than a dozen states and throughout several Caribbean Islands. The huge fortune he amassed allowed him to purchase his own island in the South of France, where he lived out his life.

T.J. Reynolds had owned the Pony Express for more than two decades. He opened his establishment with the winnings he received from gambling and horse racing. It had always been his desire to own a horse farm, and his dream had come true. With his earnings he purchased five large horse farms and hired the best trainers to groom them and prepare them for sale or racing.

He hired Sal's construction firm to design and build a modern state-of-the-art racetrack with glass enclosed VIP viewing stands, a racing museum, and trendy restaurant lounge. He fondly named his racing venue Pony Express, and it quickly became the most popular racing track in the state of Georgia. He was fortunate that a few of his horses ran in and won some of the most prestigious of racing events.

On the wall right behind the desk of Madame Butterfly's office at the Cut and Curl hung a plaque that read: "Some things never ever change - they just get better with time." This is exactly what occurred with Madame Butterfly and her love of brothels. She realized that this was her passion and she would never change - so she got better with time.

She positioned herself to manage and own a series of legal brothels throughout the state of Nevada. The difference between her brothels and others in Nevada was location. She popularized building Bed and Breakfast motels right next to her brothels. In addition to her brothels, she owned a nationwide chain of stores featuring the finest silk and linen bedroom accessories, which brought romantic inspiration into the homes of millions of Americans.

In her later years she married an ex-pimp who expanded her empire globally.

All of this was taking place when the stock markets were booming, the dollar was strong, and the overall U. S. economy supported both. It was a wonderful time for the conglomerate and its members in their choice of investments. The Big Four profits had quadrupled the $6 million made from the first year of investing, and the money continued growing with each passing month.

CJ's goal of becoming a millionaire at the age of 25 five didn't happen exactly on schedule; however, shortly thereafter his overall net worth was $5 million and counting. The total worth of b.h. conglomerate was in the neighborhood of $75 million and this was achieved in a span of just six years. CJ's dreams and lofty visions had surpassed the goals he had imagined and he and Shelly were pleased beyond belief with their collective successes.

Their celebrations included lavish trips abroad to Europe, Africa, and the Far East. There didn't seem to be any apparent obstacles in their immediate paths. Theirs was only the joy and contentment of living a good life from this high pinnacle of prosperity.

All of this was very new and humbling for CJ and it encouraged him to do expanded charitable projects for the poor and less fortunate. As a silent partner of Shelly's he started an educational foundation to support academically challenged students achieve their potential. A community youth center was established to enhance self-esteem and provide academics, counseling, values-driven business education, and entrepreneurship training and experience.

It was these qualities of giving and empathy that Shelly loved most about CJ.

Despite the seven-year stretch of successful investing and political involvement, a determined storm cloud was forming and heading their way. The aggressive campaign of the attorney general was starting to heat up and the politicians who benefitted from b.h. contributions were losing their political muscle. A broad coalition of business executives wanted the land and rights for redeveloping the Beehive district into a corporate headquarters zone. The collective capital of this new group far surpassed that of the b.h. conglomerate; in fact, the coalition of executives proposed to buy out the Beehive owners, offering an astonishing $200 million.

In order to control the political agenda of the city, they began pumping money into the politicians' coffers that far outweighed what b.h. could match. Their politicians adopted the theme of law and order, an old cliché that rallied citizens around their promise to clean up the sordid image of vice, racketeering, and graft that had been a hallmark of the

Beehive section of town. The real motive behind the new agenda, however, was money - for the politicians, the corporations, the city treasury, and themselves.

The pressures were mounting and continued to escalate every week with police raids, arrests, and closing down neighborhood establishments in the Beehive. The main objective was to break the effective control of the b.h. conglomerate.

The strategy for the attorney general was to go after the weakest members of b.h. and expose any forms of corruption he could find. This strategy proved to be harder to execute than he imagined because sitting judges and high-ranking officials frequented the Beehive.

On one night an arrest was made that proved to be most invaluable - the arrest of Bootsy, the kingpin of pimps and hustlers. He had savagely beaten and wounded one of his whores for holding out money that was due to him. The woman had been beaten many times before, but this time after recovering from her injuries in the hospital she was pressured to press charges against Bootsy.

The prosecutor for this case was working with the district attorney and trying to collect any information he could about b.h. conglomerate. He figured that if anyone knew something it would be Bootsy the pimp.

Bootsy swore to God that he didn't know anything, but he was threatened with jail time if he didn't come forward with something in a matter of a few days. It became clear to him that it would not be wise to implicate any of the principals of the Big Four, because they were all protected by Mr. Sal and his mobster clientele; if he did so, it would cost him his life. He would have to find a lesser link.

Bootsy had an ongoing conflict with Madame Butterfly because of their mutual use of girls for prostitution, and now one of her former girls was working for him. He bribed her with the promise of a reward if she could get any information about b.h.

After some time, physical threats, and emotional torture, she remembered a particular john she worked one night. He was talking about money he invested with b.h. and this young kid with all the angles and ideas about the market named CJ. This was enough information for Bootsy to get off the hook with the prosecutor, who began an investigation into CJ's business affairs.

Sal still had paid informants in the police department who eagerly forwarded any information about the course of the investigation to him. He organized a meeting with the Big Four and CJ to work out a counter plan to avoid prosecutions. The options were hotly debated: No member wanted to give up the goose that had laid their golden eggs.

CJ's suggested that he be sacrificed for the good of the whole and that they sell the b.h. conglomerate for $300 million to the corporate group that had been courting them. They would equally split the money between them and go legitimate with their already established diverse businesses.

Sal didn't like the idea at all, but was overruled by the membership. CJ comforted Sal's fears by telling him that there was no paper trail that could lead the district attorney's office anywhere. He also reinforced to Sal that his signature hadn't been applied to any corporate papers that might implicate him.

CJ's thinking for this apparent chess move was to free the Big Four from any possible indictments and to deflect the attention elsewhere. After all, they profited more than they had ever dreamed and could simply relocate to another state and live in ease and in comfort.

All of them agreed to sell and transfer to other locations except Sal. He agreed to sell but was not willing to stand by and leave CJ alone to face whatever problems may come his way; he still had some political allies that he felt he could depend on if needed.

Shelly was not in favor of the sacrificial lamb strategy. Naturally she was nervous for CJ and she could only think about the possibility of it not working. She finally relented because of CJ's calm demeanor and confidence that it could work. He informed her that their love was about to be tested, and, in the end, no matter the outcome, they would survive and surface stronger as a result of it. She agreed in theory but still had doubts about the strategy. While she vowed to stand by her man, she was unable to prepare herself for the possibility of a negative outcome.

In the course of the next year and a half the district attorney went after CJ three times. The first investigation focused on the accounting firm where he had worked. However, this scheme backfired because of CJ's meticulous accounting skills and record keeping.

Not long after that incident, the district attorney became aware of the properties owned by Shelly and CJ in the Poconos. He charged CJ with money laundering as the source of obtaining the land and the buildings but failed because the defense proved through a paper trail the money was partially Shelly's as CJ's silent partner and the rest was loaned to them from her father's enterprises.

CJ foresaw this coming two years in advance and on the counseling of Shelly began to deposit millions of dollars into off-shore accounts in Belize, Panama, and Switzerland. All of these locations were tax havens from the U.S. government and couldn't be traced or investigated by the Internal Revenue Service. Once again a jury couldn't convict him due to a lack of credible evidence, and so he was acquitted.

The next trial was bogus right from the beginning. CJ was to be tried in front of the same judge who presided at the previous trial. Although his defense team complained that it was a conflict of interest, the judge refused to recuse himself and ordered the trial to go forward.

This time the district attorney had given misleading information to the Securities and Exchange Commission. Based on a tip from the DA, the SEC investigated CJ's financial activities in an effort to find evidence of insider trading. Like many such cases, the evidence on possible insider trading the SEC collected was circumstantial. The agency, however, decided to file charges.

When the case went to trial, the district attorney falsely claimed there was a corroborating witness. The witness, however, never made an appearance in the courtroom.

Although the case for the prosecution turned out to be weak, based on circumstantial evidence with no corroborating witnesses, neither the judge nor the jury could entertain the idea that CJ at his age could be so knowledgeable about the stock market – or that lucky. They were convinced that someone must have given him some inside information about certain stocks in order for him to make millions in a short span of time.

The defense team for CJ refuted this claim and maintained that there was no basis for the allegations because his signature or name never appeared on any documents related to b.h. Inc. The DA, enraged, decided to attack his character because of his close association with a known felon with possible mafia connections, Sal Nardone.

Sal wasn't a target of this investigation, but his association with CJ was being called into question. It wasn't a secret that the two of them enjoyed a friendly game of chess every week at Dee Dee's Lounge and always in front of many witnesses. It also was common knowledge the two never talked business there. In order to gather dirt on CJ, the DA got permission to wiretap his phone.

Those close to Sal and CJ could have advised the DA to save his energy, because the two were careful not to discuss any deals over the phone.

Since the wiretap failed to produce dirt on CJ, the DA did not introduce it into evidence.

The DA's final move to nail CJ was to call as a witness the beaten and bruised whore who worked for Bootsy. She claimed under oath that she wouldn't reveal the name of the john who was the source of her accusations because he was a high-ranking political official and she didn't want to tarnish his name or reputation.

Naturally, the defense objected, arguing that conversations between whores and their johns are not privileged communication. The judge brazenly overruled their objection and the defense team was forced to adopt a strategy of discrediting the witness.

Under cross examination they attempted to establish that her statements were unreliable at best and her credibility was questionable because of her business relationship with Bootsy.

It was obvious to many that the DA was using this case as a political tool to bolster his status within the judicial system. They believed it was important for him to be viewed as a law and order DA doing his bit to clean up a criminally infected area.

Sal's sources dug deeper and learned that the DA was vying for an appointment as an appellate court judge. The informants also told Sal that the jury may have been tainted; they had heard that at least two or three jurors were handpicked or possibly paid for by the corporate group that wanted the jury to render a guilty verdict against CJ.

This information was eventually given to the defense team, but they had run out of time to substantiate the allegations of judicial misconduct and jury tampering and introduce this new evidence. They decided that if CJ was convicted they would appeal, citing documented irregularities that occurred during the trial.

Throughout the trial CJ was very calm and composed; he never showed the slightest concern. It was his nature and personality to be calm, however, the prosecutors and judge viewed this attitude as smugness on his part, which reinforced their preconception that he was hiding something.

Anna and Shelly were nervous as the trial was drawing to an end - and Sal was suspicious of the DA and the court proceedings. As both sides delivered their closing arguments, the mood in the courtroom was tense, and the jurors gave no indication of which side they believed.

The jury deliberated for only three hours before re-entering the court room. The judge asked CJ to stand and then asked the jury foreman to read the verdict. The verdict he announced was guilty on the charge of insider trading.

Immediately a gasp of disbelief rose throughout the courtroom. Anna and Shelly sobbed. Others shouted "Fix" and "No!"

The judge pounded his gavel and demanded the court regain silence and come to order. He announced the verdict to CJ again and ordered him to return to the court for sentencing in two weeks. CJ was released to his lawyers, who immediately made a formal statement that an appeal would be filed.

Shelly and Anna made their way to the front of the courtroom to embrace CJ. As they cried in his arms, he returned their hugs and said, "Don't worry, this is only check; it is not checkmate."

CHAPTER 12

The 13ᵗʰ

In the aftermath of the two week trial - the second in a period of less than two years - all parties involved with CJ needed a full exhale, reflection, and reload for the upcoming appeal.

The defense team for CJ was fully confident that there was more than sufficient evidence to overturn the verdict, albeit that would take some time.

Anna was distraught that her son had been convicted of a crime and she couldn't understand how and why it had come to this. All she could think about was that it must be a mistake. She was, however, starting to panic as to whether she would ever see her only loving child again or be able to run her fingers through his curly hair and hold him near.

This was not the case for Shelly. She remained optimistically hopeful, masking her nervousness about the complexities of the trial, their future, and the outcome of this new setback.

There was never any thought of abandoning the appeal nor was there the least doubt about CJ's absolute innocence. It was Shelly's unyielding love for CJ that kept her strong and focused. She had always been a fighter, a Texan, and she was ready to rumble. She contacted her father and after a long and intense discussion they agreed to form a legal defense team to tackle the appellate case. Her father was very connected to and involved with some of the nation's most powerful politicians, many of whom owed him favors for their campaign contributions. The list of some of these powerful men would include senators, governors, and heads of federal agencies.

Although Shelly was a daddy's girl and his only child, she was fiercely independent and rarely asked for favors. Throughout her adult life they continued to maintain a close and loving relationship both professionally and personally. He reassured her that he would assemble the best legal minds available and there wasn't any cost they could not bear.

Shelly was relieved to hear this, but didn't mention it to CJ, because she was well aware of his pride and his sense of independence.

Shelly's mind was working overtime with ideas of how she could help. She finally decided to hire a very crafty but effective private investigator to look into the background of this seemingly corrupt trial judge and district attorney. In whatever time was left before the day of sentencing, all she wanted to do was make love with CJ. And with each passing hour spent together that is exactly what they did.

As for CJ, he analyzed everything through the lens of a chess match and thought there were moves to be made for a comeback victory. He didn't appear to be fazed by any of the court proceedings. He took everything in stride and remained confident. He absolutely believed that being stressed or depressed wasn't an option for him and he was determined to find a key that would turn the staggering results around.

CJ was fond of saying that karma exists in this world and that if you do good works they will return to benefit you.

He returned to his job at the accounting firm to sort out his office and surprisingly was received warmly and supportively by his coworkers. They all thanked him for his years of service and success at the firm and pledged their continued support in the upcoming appeal. Everyone at the firm thought he was being railroaded and wished him strength going forward as he sought to find justice in his case.

The optimism displayed by CJ was definitely not shared by everyone, and his mentor, Sal, declared he would take a different approach to resolving this dilemma. To Mr. Sal, the guilty verdict was a pronouncement of war on his protégé and business partner and he took it very personally.

Sal was a hard knock product from the streets of Brooklyn and even though he now resided in New Jersey, he never forgot how to fight dirty and win. During the questionable trial, Sal foresaw that the outcome wasn't going toward justice or fairness, so he began preparing a strategy of using his own unique style of investigating.

He was keenly aware that most men in positions of power had a hidden past or present that they would rather keep secret from the public. He felt something strange about the relationship between the judge and the district attorney and questioned why the same man was allowed to preside over both trials.

Sal decided to spread a little money around to local snitches and pay rolled informants. In the underworld circuits this is known as a bounty; the reward money would be given to whoever produces the most damaging and creditable evidence on this judge. Everyone knew they couldn't derail the sentencing deadline; the gathering of this information was to help the appellate court.

The Big Four establishments in the Beehive always kept records on the most important people who frequented their illegal businesses. This was done in an effort to protect them from prosecution if they were ever arrested or needed a favor. It was Madame Butterfly and the owner of the Sugar Cane nightclub who would provide the most damaging evidence against this judge. The other members of the Big Four also pledged to give their support to CJ; after he was responsible for the prosperity they had all achieved.

It was November and seasonal change from life to death was evident all around. The leaves on the trees were dying, drying, and changing colors. The temperatures were brisker and getting colder and the daytime sunlight was shortened with each passing day. It was an ironic metaphor for the changes that were about to happen in CJ's life.

Shelly and CJ did everything they could to avoid anger or depression. It seemed as though they were spending more time together, now that time was winding down. One early Sunday afternoon while taking a leisurely stroll hand in hand through New York's Central Park; CJ stopped momentarily to ask Shelly a question: "What do you believe to be the most precious gift that God has given us?" Shelly thought about the question for a moment and then said:

"I don't know; I guess it would be love or life. What do you think, honey?"

"I believe the answer to that question would be time."

Shelly could sense that he was doing some serious thinking and reflecting and she waited patiently as he continued to elaborate on the question. There was an empty park bench nearby and he gently took her hand and beckoned her to sit. Shelly's eyes were fixed on the calm demeanor and soft smile upon his face and she didn't know what to expect.

CJ kissed her long and slow before he went on to further explain. He had been reading books about Eastern philosophies for more than a year and now his consciousness was reflecting a newly formed understanding about values and truth. He had never become a member of any religion, sect, or cult as a younger man, and yet his values and open humanity had led him to widely accept different spiritual paths.

He was studying and reading books about Buddhism, Judaism, Islam, and Hinduism. The insight of their prophets and teachers revealed to him that their central concepts and values were one and the same. He confidently shared his new awareness with Shelly, because they had very similar concepts of truth. CJ would occasionally discuss such themes with Shelly by spontaneous questions and answers.

"I believe that time is governed and connected to all created things by God," he said. "I can see its relevance in life, death, health, and how it functions throughout the entire universe. Without time there is no growth, order, and structure in our lives and we live aimlessly without purpose. Time is a token granted to us; we cannot control it, nor can we exist without it. Once we lose it, we cannot regain it - and if we misuse time it may recoil against us and cause further disruptions in our lives. It is a precious gift that cannot be denied and a blessing whenever we use it righteously."

Shelly was smiling and then breathed a long, slow exhale.

"I agree honey; time is a gift and must be used with love and care. And no matter what comes between or happens to us, if we invest our time for more love and peace, it will return to us better than it was invested. I understand, CJ, and my time with you is my love for you."

Shelly squeezed his hands, feeling the warmth and the strength of his heart; she was communicating deeply with CJ without using harmful words such as jail, prison, or separation.

As they stood and continued their strolling through the park, Shelly noticed through the trees a sliver of sun slowly setting into the horizon. "Look!" she said. "There is time; moving on, moving forward."

"Yes," replied CJ, "and here we are joined together by time."

They continued to walk toward Shelly's home to enjoy an evening of lovemaking until the stars appeared in the brilliant night sky.

The weather for the day of sentencing was forecast to be cloudy with a slight chance of rain, but when CJ arrived it cleared and the sun came out. Could this have been another sign or metaphor, he wondered. That was how he envisioned it, which allowed him to have a positive attitude despite the trouble and turmoil facing him.

Slowly the small courtroom began to fill up with an assortment of spectators, friends, and coworkers, all present to give hope and support for CJ. Many of them came up to him offering their well wishes and for him to keep his head up.

All of the members of the Big Four were there for one last look at the judge who they believed held the blame for the trial and outcome. They vowed to one day return to this very courtroom after compiling information on the judge and witness him sentenced for his crimes.

The last ones to enter the courtroom before the arrival of the judge were Anna, Shelly, and her father.

Shelly's father had been in the corridor conversing with the new defense team; he wanted them to witness the sentencing and file immediately for an appeal.

"All rise," said the bailiff, as the judge took his seat and asked for CJ to please come forward.

Looking over his glasses at CJ and he announced: "Charles Jesus Sinclair, you have been convicted of insider trading violations as defined by the Securities and Exchange Commission and hereby will be committed to serve a sentence of three to five years for this criminal offense. On this 20th day of November you will be sent to the United States Penitentiary, Lewisburg, and immediately begin to serve a minimum of two and a half years before possible parole.

"Bailiff, please remove the prisoner and begin the process."

Shelly broke down crying and ran to give CJ one long, lasting hug and kiss. As the bailiff separated them and clamped the handcuffs onto CJ's wrist he smiled and said to Shelly, "I love you baby."

Anna was stunned, shocked, and in disbelief; she quickly looked around in search of Shelly. After watching Shelly sobbing, she too began to cry. The two embraced each other as long and as hard as they could, each one trying to offer whatever emotional comfort they could muster.

The stunned observers within the courtroom, refusing to believe what they heard, began yelling and shouting in protest, to the dismay of the judge and prosecutors. The judge was completely caught off guard by the anger and noise of this rowdy crowd and quickly made an exit from the bench.

A bewildered CJ stood with tears forming in his eyes, blowing soft kisses to Anna and Shelly.

The bailiff removed him from the courtroom.

Processing procedures took about three hours, after which CJ boarded a prison bus loaded with convicted felons, all headed to the U.S. Penitentiary in Lewisburg, Pennsylvania.

Lewisburg was nearly a three hour drive away, and located in a remote rural section of Pennsylvania. Built in the 1930s the federal maximum-security prison is reserved for prisoners convicted of the most serious crimes. It housed those convicted of white-collar crimes such as tax evasion and embezzlement as well as some of the most vicious criminals in society. It was not uncommon for murderers and rapist to be jailed at Lewisburg.

The prison was never overcrowded and contained farms, machine shops, and manufacturing plants for labor purposes and rehabilitation.

The journey to Lewisburg was an adventure in many ways for CJ. He wore chains and braces around his ankles and his handcuffs were attached to a chain that led down to a bolted bar on the floor. The discomfort was unbearable and the constant staring and checking of their chains by the three shotgun carrying guards made it worse. The only compensation was his window seat, which allowed him to look out upon the passing cars and landscape and release his mind from the harsh reality of those chains.

Finally, they arrived, and that meant a whole new beginning. There were mugshot photos to be taken and fingerprint processing before the arriving prisoners received their new identification. The new identification included a 10-digit number, a prison-issued jumpsuit, and a place to be confined in, known as the cell.

The transition from civilian life to prison life was all designed to reinforce the reality that one's citizenship and human rights have been restricted or removed.

The mundane routines of being counted several times daily, the restricted times for showers, meals, and the brief allotted time to get fresh air are all designed to remind inmates that their lives are no longer their own. It is a system of cruel control and repression designed to lead to dehumanization.

For CJ, the first night was the hardest; he barely slept, and when he attempted to relax all he could think of was the life he led before this. The confining cell housed only him, and the bars at the entrance were a constant reminder of his captivity. The number one consolation was a small window near the ceiling that allowed a glimpse of sunlight to enter for a small portion of the day.

The discipline required to counter these forms of regular oppression comes from a deep place inside one's head and heart. CJ continued to remind himself at various times daily that he was doing the time and that he wouldn't let it do him. For the most part he kept to himself and rarely spoke to anyone about anything. After two or three months following a disciplined routine and adjusting to the rigors of life behind bars, there was an opening and things began to change.

One day while eating in the mess hall, he opened up and returned a conversation with a man sitting nearby. This small, muscular inmate politely introduced himself as Little Wayne Sesto. He was incarcerated for a series of crimes, including kidnapping, murder, bribery, and extortion. The name Little Wayne was bestowed upon him by the prison guards because of his stature and because he was serving only a 12-year sentence for the crimes of which he had been convicted. Although small in height, Wayne had a big reputation at Lewisburg and very little tolerance for bullies twice his size. On a few occasions he sent bullies to the infirmary for treatment resulting from serious injuries.

Before being incarcerated, Little Wayne worked as a debt collector and enforcer for a Mafia family in Philadelphia.

After the introductions and pleasantry exchanges with CJ, Little Wayne leaned in closer to interrupt the conversation and in a whisper said, "I have a message for you from your friend Mr. Sal."

Surprised to hear this, CJ asked, "Do you know Mr. Sal?"

"Yes I do, we have been good friends for years and during my youth we worked a couple of jobs together. I only have a few minutes, so listen carefully and keep all that I say to you to yourself.

"Sal pulled a few strings from his political connections and there will be a few changes made while you're here - for your protection, comfort. He has asked and paid me and my associates to be your shadow and keep you from harm. Your cell will be changed and you will be moved next to my cell and there will be some amenities added to your cell for personal comfort. In a week, you will have a job working at the library - one of the best jobs to have in prison. You'll have access to all reading materials. And lastly Mr. Sal sent you a small chess board with pieces so you can play when we get yard time.

"All of these changes have been coordinated with the warden's permission, so don't worry about anything. Mr. Sal is an important man with loyal friends in high places and he has informed me of your relationship over the years. He has made this decision to ensure you're taken care of while here at Lewisburg. My advice for you is to accept all that he has arranged.

"And oh! By the way, he said he will be here in a few weeks to see how you are doing."

CJ was shocked, but grateful for the friendship of Sal and his connections. He thanked Little Wayne just as the whistles blew ending their lunch period. All the prisoners were lined up, checked for weapons, and marshalled back to their restricted cells.

This time CJ was anxious to return to his cell because he wanted to read the mail that was delivered earlier; it was the one time when he could find tranquility by reading bi-weekly mail received from Anna or Shelly.

He was not allowed to have visitors for the first two months, but when the ban was lifted, Shelly was the first to visit. Her first visit was a strange one and she had to endure many restrictions. Her long drive was followed by the detailed searching procedures, and finally she was constrained from any personal contact and could only talk from behind a glass barrier by phone. It was challenging and required some patience and much discipline, but it didn't matter to Shelly because she would have climbed any mountain to see or touch him.

Shelly incorporated into her weekly schedule a visit to Lewisburg to spend what amounted to a 10-minute, phone-to-phone visit.

As time went by CJ became more accustomed to the rules and regulations of prison life, and, as he showed full compliance, the visitation restrictions were lifted and he was able to receive Shelly with fewer barriers.

The joy of her visits was always the stolen touch they were not supposed to have. In between her weekly visits, she would write him encouraging love letters and poetry to keep his spirits lifted.

After his seventh month of incarceration, his need to see her increased. He reversed his decision of seeing her in person and asked her to write letters instead. He couldn't stomach her visiting him in that condition any more and with every visit it became increasingly more difficult whenever she was gone.

She complied with his request despite her disagreement, and she increased her letter writing as a compromise.

Whenever Sal visited CJ, he brought with him any updated news concerning the appeal process and the progress being made. This was always a confidence booster for CJ and gave him the encouragement needed to remain optimistic. Sal had arranged for his cell to be changed and he was allowed a radio, a rug, and specially cooked meals delivered during the holiday seasons for him and Little Wayne.

The hardest times in prison are the holidays of Thanksgiving and Christmas. These were special occasions when the opportunity to spend intimate time with family, friends, and loved ones were at a premium. Because of the connections with the prison guards, and a little bribery, Sal was able to have a delicious turkey dinner sent in at Thanksgiving and a small pine tree covered with decorations during the December holidays.

All prisoners are not equal. There are and have always been two types of people that are incarcerated. The first type is a bona-fide criminal and social undesirable who cannot be rehabilitated and therefore should remain in prison. The second type is a redeemable person who represents an error in judgement or a miscarriage of justice. They may have been prosecuted for political reasons or unable to afford good attorneys. Not all of those who are locked away are animals, criminals, or misfit individuals; there are some who are actually innocent and shouldn't be there. CJ was intelligent enough to recognize the difference between the two extremes and he balanced his associating with inmates based on that premise.

The library job turned out to be a blessing. It allowed CJ the freedom to escape from the monotony of prison life. Through self-discipline he was learning to be free by immersing his mind into a book to learn something new or travel a road in time or space by reading a novel. It wasn't physical work, and he was paid a monthly stipend for sorting, cataloging, and delivering books, magazines, or newspapers to the inmates and staff.

The library was where and how he befriended an inmate who, too, was educated and well read. One day while CJ was returning books into their appropriate shelf places he slipped on the recently mopped floor, and, while trying to balance himself, banged into a shelf, sending books flying into the air. The inmate who was mopping the floor heard the commotion, came right over, and offered to give CJ a hand.

"Hey! Are you all right? Let me give you a hand."

"Thanks," CJ replied. "I'm fine now. I just didn't see the wet floor sign."

"My name is Ahmed; what's yours?"

"They call me CJ and I work here in the library."

The two men shook hands and started a typical conversation about how they both arrived at Lewisburg.

Ahmed was a young man from South Africa. He had migrated to America along with his family to avoid apartheid many years earlier. He grew up in the city of Philadelphia and his intentions were to pursue a college education in the field of agricultural science and development.

He had arrived at Lewisburg as the result of a manslaughter conviction for defending his sister from a group of racist white men who attacked her verbally and physically just because she was wearing a Muslim head covering. He was successful and defeated the men who attacked her. Unfortunately, one of the men died from head wounds and two others were hospitalized with multiple broken bones and other assorted injuries.

Ahmed was well known throughout his community as a black belt martial artist in the discipline of Kung Fu. The prosecution declared that his hands and feet were registered as lethal weapons and then the all-white, male jury found him guilty of first degree manslaughter. He received a sentence of seven years and had served only two.

Ahmed worked as a maintenance man at Lewisburg. He was the quiet type who primarily kept to himself, loved reading all types of books, and practiced diligently the art of Kung Fu in his prison cell.

As the two shared an open conversation about their lives and court cases, they began to realize how much they had in common. It wasn't long before they developed a tight-knit relationship that lasted far beyond their time in prison. They would look out for one another, sharing knowledge from books or exchanging stories about their youthful lives - and sometimes enjoying a friendly game of chess.

If Ahmed represented the redeemable prototype prisoner, then Little Wayne was the exact opposite. He remained loyal to Mr. Sal and shielded CJ from the brutalities of everyday prison life.

On several occasions CJ wrote to Shelly describing the inhumane treatment he witnessed or heard about: the frequent and violent sodomy rapes during the night, the occasional stabbings and use of handmade weapons on one another, and the regular beatings of guards against the inmates and vice versa. It was the past and present violent reputation of little Wayne, his connections with the guards, and Sal's payroll allowance that kept CJ safe and away from all of the violence, intimidation, and abusive behavior.

Little Wayne was a by-product of prison life and before that of street life; there was little room for reform or redemption. Everyone knew that if ever he was released, the Philadelphia Mafia had a job waiting for him on the outside. He belonged to them and they to him.

There was one incident that made a lasting impression on CJ. It occurred on a cloudy, rainy afternoon during lunch time in the mess hall. The two most vicious gangs at Lewisburg began a distraction that escalated into a melee and as a result left two inmates and one prison guard dead.

It started when two inmates stood up at opposite ends of a long lunch table and began cursing at each other. They began to approach one another as the officers moved in to restore order. As soon as the first guard was 5 feet away from one of the cursing men the scene repeated itself about five tables away in the opposite direction.

The distraction took place on both sides of the mess hall to separate the guards and the melee took place in the middle.

The first officer to approach the loudest cursing inmate was jumped from behind and violently knocked to the floor. It was clear to little Wayne and CJ, who were watching attentively, that the primary target was that first officer. When the officer was knocked down and inmates started to stomp on him that was the cue for mass confusion and mayhem. At that Instant, the mess hall erupted into a full scale riot with fighting between guards and inmates throughout.

Little Wayne didn't hesitate for a moment; he had seen this type of scene before. He quickly turned over a lunch table, and, using it as a barrier, he grabbed CJ by the collar and dragged him toward the nearest wall. They were squatting low and moved toward the wall, while trying to avoid being hit by flying debris or clubs.

The loud screaming and yelling was deafening and soon there was blood splattered everywhere. The bells and emergency alarms were sounded, and that meant the National Guard would soon storm the building, which would lead to more casualties.

CJ was visibly shaken and very nervous, but Wayne was cool and calm. He told CJ to lie on the floor and keep his head down while he covered him and wait until the militia came into the hall.

Within minutes the troops stormed into the mess hall, firing overhead and yelling for the inmates to lie face down on the floor.

The mess hall was in complete disarray and people were crying for help and assistance. As the noise settled and quietness prevailed the militia lined up the prisoners and marched them by gun-point back to their cells.

The warden ordered a full investigation as to the cause of the riot and in the meantime the prison was on full lockdown with no yard or other privileges for two weeks.

The investigation showed that a guard had smuggled drugs into the prison and was selling them to a gang. This upset the balance of gang power and influence, and, as a result, the guard lost his life. The prison riot sent 23 inmates to the infirmary with various bruises and wounds; but it also sent two to the cemetery.

CJ didn't inform Shelly about the riot for nearly a month. He didn't want her alarmed about his safety; but when he did tell her she already knew about it. Shelly was nobody's fool; she had arranged her Intel network to check on CJ's safety and health while he was at Lewisburg.

Since the earliest days of his youth whenever a state of stress or trouble entered his life, the one asset that served him and allowed him to escape was reading a novel or history book. Reading seemed to lift him upon a magic carpet and carry him far away. It would come to his aid once again at this stressed period in his life and with it would come a new friend, Ahmed.

There are always loopholes in any system, regardless of how it is structured, and CJ managed to slip away from his daily library duties for some reading or sharing knowledge with his friend. It was a pathway for them to broaden the mind, discover the unknown, and stretch their personal education.

CJ discovered the life and times of Malcolm X, the repressive system of apartheid, and a new awareness of the struggles of civil and human rights. Ahmed discovered the numerous inventions and valued assets brought to the world from the minds of slaves.

Although he was born in South Africa and a product of biracial parenting, Ahmed knew very little of the great African civilizations and empires that once ruled and taught the world. Together they learned from famous African American authors, poets, playwrights, and a long list of world-renowned actors and musicians.

Whenever they'd met at the library or other hideaways, it became a special time of peace and refuge for both.

On one of those particular meetings, Ahmed said he had discovered something intriguing while reading the United States constitution. It was the written words of The 13th Amendment to the United States Constitution_that shocked his senses and opened his eyes to a new and indifferent reality.

Neither slavery nor involuntary servitude, except as a punishment for crime whereof the party shall have been duly convicted, shall exist within the United States, or any place subject to their jurisdiction.

Ahmed showed this to CJ and they read it repeatedly and out loud; they looked at each other and then, said in unison: "Slavery still exists, and we are the new slaves."

Laughter followed, but, surely it was no laughing matter. As they regained seriousness they continued to read more about how the 13th Amendment hadn't abolished slavery at all, but rather modified it to live and thrive in U.S. prisons. Initially it was a hard pill to swallow, so they decided to do further research concerning the prison- industrial complex and what they learned was even more devastating.

The basis of this complex is the same belief that initiated the institution of U.S. slavery: the dehumanization and criminalization of being a non-white and primarily male in the case of incarceration, both for the purpose of creating a free labor supply.

From further reading and research, they uncovered another fact: that many American companies took full advantage shortly after ratifying the 13th Amendment - along with the government - to criminalize the poor and primarily Black populations for profit.

CJ and Ahmed were affected deeply and humiliated by this new knowledge and they pledged in the name of God Almighty to do whatever they could to wake up people and to spread the word. They naively thought that, if more people were aware of the 13th Amendment, they would avoid becoming a slave by going to prison.

The most ironic aspect they found was that the entire the 13th Amendment is less than 50 words - and much isn't about abolishing or ending slavery. The core issue was how to morph slavery into a different format while maintaining its value of a free and prosperous labor market. This insight and the lie that their history classes had taught would haunt them for the rest of their lives; but it did not deter them from pursuing their research, which would reward their efforts. They vowed to get as much information as possible about the relationships between corporations, the U.S. government, and those who are responsible for creating laws that trap and imprison the poor and people of color.

Although it was a relief to read and learn new things, sometimes it felt like the information they exposed was a curse, because it seemed to leave them powerless to do anything about it. Learning while being confined and powerless could also be the seeds for depression and despair. CJ could be drawn to solace and inspiration whenever the slightest hint of despair would taunt him by receiving a letter or a phone call from Shelly.

He had written to her about the developing friendship and comradery of Ahmed and how he was opening up to spiritual pathways that previously were unimportant to him.

He had also learned a very valuable lesson - that friendship could often lead to your needs being answered. In his most recent letter to Shelly, he informed her that he was reading the Bible as often as possible and that he had discovered a different spiritual source and complement to the essence of the Bible; it was a new book for him but not to the world. It was entitled The Quran.

He was delighted to mention that he was learning the true value of prayer and silent meditations, and how much he yearned for a time when they could enhance their connection of love, through prayer and joined meditations.

Night time was when he did most of his writing; it was as though he was giving her a goodnight kiss just before going to sleep. It was also the most peaceful time for him to do so, with his work illuminated by a battery-operated lamp Sal had delivered to him.

There were other times when CJ found it a very profitable habit to read her letters at night; it would be akin to taking a hot sedative for sleep and dreaming until the morning light creeped into his cell. One such night as his head lay down on his pillow and he gazed up at the ceiling, he opened Shelly's letter.

Staring at him in bold print, he read: "Thank God, I've got some good news!"

CJ sprang up on his bunk with wide-eyed anticipation and began reading aloud softly.

It was a seven-page letter with full details concerning the investigators' findings about the judge, the DA, and the corporate group, Magnet Inc. It was Magnet that needed the land for their proposal to rehabilitate the Beehive section. They also needed the political credit for destroying CJ and making him an example before going after some others.

A broad smile appeared upon his face as he read the details about how this incriminating evidence would be very significant in the appeal process, overturning his guilty verdict and setting him free.

Shelly's letter described the judge's illicit activities with prostitutes at Madame Butterfly's Beehive brothel. Madame Butterfly kept check receipts and had sexually explicit pictures of the judge with one of her most popular whores.

There was also the discovery that the judge was on the Magnet Inc. payroll as a board member. These two situations would have been sufficient for him to have recused himself from the trial. The case was a setup from its initiation and CJ was the target.

Shelly also wrote that there was proof of jury tampering. Sal Nardone had learned that two of the jurors were paid by Magnet Inc. to deliver the decisive vote of guilty that convicted CJ and sent him to prison.

All of these disclosures - along with the inconsistences and lack of credible witnesses during the trial - would certainly be enough new information for an appeal and the possible overturning of his conviction.

The final note in Shelly's letter was that the lawyers would submit their applications of proof to the appellate court. They would come to visit CJ after filing their motion for an appeal and explain the next move in the process. Shelly had been informed by the lawyers, and her dad said CJ might be released in as little as two months, she wrote.

After reading the letter twice CJ put his head in his hands; he was crying, and he began to pray, thanking Almighty God for His favors and imploring God for patience until the matter was finally settled.

The next day Shelly Called CJ and said she really needed to see him before his possible release. She said she had a huge surprise that couldn't wait any longer, and requested a visitation within a few days.

It had been a little more than a year since she last saw him or touched his hand. CJ was feeling so good from reading her most recent letter that he immediately said yes. They both sounded excited by the reply and they kept repeating to each other, "I love you! I love you!" until the time ran out and the call was sadly interrupted.

That night both CJ and Shelly slept soundly and peacefully as they both dreamt about a long-awaited visit to see and touch one another once again.

CHAPTER 13

Free at last

Sunday afternoons are the busiest for prison visitation throughout most areas of the country. This day is often referred to as family day. It is a day when more children, wives, and relatives come to visit and/or leave packages for the inmates.

The lawyers representing CJ made a special request to the warden for an extended visitation for Shelly. The warden reviewed the extenuating circumstance put forth by the lawyers and granted Shelly a conjugal visit.

This information was kept hidden from CJ until the time his visit was announced. The lieutenant who came to escort CJ to a private room explained that the warden had reviewed his files and felt he deserved to receive this kind of special privilege.

The conjugal visitation section of the prison was unfamiliar to CJ, and the walk there was farther than he imagined. They arrived at last and the lieutenant winked and bid him to have a good time.

CJ cautiously opened the door, and there, sitting and on a couch was his beloved Shelly, smiling.

"Oh my God," said CJ as he quickly moved toward her for an embrace; then he paused and realized a baby was nestled in her arms. He braced one arm around her back and the other around the little boy. He showered her with compliments on how good she looked and smelled before asking, "Who is this fine young boy?"

Shelly, beaming with joy, replied, "Take a long, hard look and you tell me; who does he look like?"

CJ took a long look. He ran his fingers through the child's wavy hair and then held him in his arms ever closer. He was looking at this beautiful child, smiling with his eyes wide open.

He started to laugh and said, "He looks like me, but how, when, and why didn't you tell me?"

"Hold on, baby; one question at a time. First put him down and let me hold you and kiss you and then I'll explain everything.

"Oh, OK, baby, but, look at him!"

"I have," said Shelly, "carefully, every day for more than 11 months. This is our son. We both belong to you, and we are family."

With that said they came together, hugging and kissing, with the little tan boy looking on. That was the first passionate kiss CJ had with Shelly since the last time they made love. After catching their breath and laughing, Shelly said: "Sit down my love, and let me start from the beginning."

"It happened on the last night that we made love, which was the night before the sentencing. The love making we shared was long, intense, and the most passionate that I had ever experienced in my life. You were very strong that night. I could barely catch my breath.

"Finally we laid there sweating and panting together for about 25 minutes before either of us moved into another position. I felt euphoria come over me and I realized at that moment that I was going to be pregnant.

"I didn't tell you about it because you told me you didn't want me seeing you in the condition of a caged animal anymore. I thought it was a sign from God, since we were separated, not to cause more stress while you were incarcerated.

"I talked this over with Anna and she thought as I did that telling you it could cause more problems than solve. We both agreed that it would add to the list of daily concerns and problems that you were already trying to handle.

"The last reason is that I have been praying daily and building a strong personal relationship with God Almighty. He has told me through dreams and inspiration that you would be coming home soon and at that time our lives could begin anew as a complete family.

"I love you, honey. I am your rock and you are mine and nothing else in this world means more to me than you and our son."

CJ was dumbstruck and tears began to swell. He just stared at Shelly in amazement and pride, pulling her closer, with the baby between them.

"You all are my love, my joy, and my comfort forevermore," he said. "I love you with every breath I take and every step I make."

They hugged tightly and warmly, and then Shelly said, "By the way, his name is Ihsan Jesus Sinclair and I brought you a copy of his birth certificate."

CJ was surprised to hear his name, and with a puzzled expression, he asked, "How did you come up with that name?"

"Well, said Shelly, I wanted to give him a name that was different and important, and while carrying him one day I stopped at a bookstore and on a shelf I noticed a book, entitled Exotic and Non-traditional Names. I purchased the book and randomly opened to a page, and there it was staring me in the face. The name is an Arabic word and it applies to both genders, and its meaning is dual. The first meaning is: 'one who does well for others,' and the second meaning is 'the person who sees God looking at him at all times, and if he doesn't see God, then he must realize that Almighty God is watching!'

"I think it will give us a platform to raise him by, and a path that he can strive to follow," she continued. "I gave him Jesus, because it is your middle name and speaks to your spirituality. What do you think?"

"I think you are brilliant and the most courageous person I've ever known," CJ responded. "I am so blessed to have you in my life, and now we share an inseparable bond between us that will forever allow us to be whole, noble, and one."

The visitation time was only for an hour and a half, so they spent the remaining time touching, looking, and kissing between moments of conversation.

Shelly kept the last surprise hidden until right before the lieutenant returned. She lifted the baby from the couch and asked CJ to stand at one end of the room while she positioned her and the baby at the other. Shelly gently put the baby in a standing position before her; then told CJ to lift his arms and call Ihsan toward him.

CJ did as he was instructed and little Ihsan walked toward his dad, smiling all the way.

CJ lifted his son into his arms, grabbed Shelly, and began vigorously kissing them both on the mouth and cheeks. At that moment there was a knock on the door; it was time for CJ to return to his cell. He was ready, but only after introducing his family to the Lieutenant and kissing Shelly and Ihsan goodbye.

This was the first time since arriving at Lewisburg that CJ felt human, connected, and liberated, and able to smile whole heartedly. He was feeling the glory of God smiling upon him, and was humbled by the thought that it wouldn't be too long before he was free.

Three weeks had passed since he received his family visit and he was still feeling happy and content from that blessing. He wrote a very personal letter to the warden to thank him for the opportunity and privilege of a conjugal visitation. It wasn't to shine up to the warden, but a way to show God the gratitude and given Him praises.

One day while working at the library, CJ received an unexpected visit. He hurried to the area for visitation and discovered his legal team and Shelly's father waiting for him. The lawyers had documented information that could be used to file an appeal, overturn the verdict, and hasten his release. The following is a list of the major charges against the judge who sat for the case.

1. Twenty-two reasonable objections were denied.
2. The judge refused to accept evidence that supported the position of the defense.
3. The judge served on a previously tried case against CJ.
4. An investigation by the ethics division of the justice department found the judge was a paid board member of Magnet Inc. and should have recused himself from hearing the case.
5. The judge colluded with Magnet Inc. to make payments to two jurors (jury tampering).
6. Illegal gambling and debt markers on file from the Sugar Cane and records of the judge consorting with prostitutes from Cut and Curl. (Pictures and cancelled checks on file were found.)

The investigators also found damaging information on the prosecutor and the district attorney; however the most important concerns for CJ's legal team were the actions and decisions of the judge.

In addition, CJ had been a model prisoner who had already served nearly two years of his five-year term, and if the appeal was unsuccessful he would be eligible for parole.

The final good news was a scheduled date in two weeks for him to appear before the appellate court.

He was extremely pleased to see Shelly's father and he thanked him and the lawyers for what they had accomplished.

Two days before his scheduled court date, CJ visited Ahmed for what he hoped would be the last time in Lewisburg. They exchanged mailing addresses and vowed to stay in touch, no matter the outcome. CJ told Ahmed he was grateful to have met him and he knew their seemingly random encounter had happened only by the will of Almighty God.

He thanked Little Wayne for his due diligence in protecting him and the wisdom he taught him about day-to-day survival in prison.

The warden and CJ sat down for their final consultation the day before he departed. It was a frank discussion about the choices we make and opportunities that we sometimes miss. The warden acknowledged the fact that CJ had been an admirable prisoner and he felt that he didn't belong in a maximum-security prison. He urged him to use his intelligence wisely and to take care of his family - to move on positively with his life and take advantage of opportunities for good.

The warden ended the conversation with an extended handshake. "There will be a car waiting for you in 30 minutes, and this suit was left here for you by Shelly," he said. "She seems like a fine young lady; be good to her."

The two shook hands and said their final good bye.

The day in court was a physical reminder for CJ of the judicial system and how it sometimes doesn't achieve justice. He took a deep breath, said a brief prayer, and readied himself for the outcome.

The entire court procedure took less than 30 minutes. The judge asked CJ to stand and then read his decision:

"It is the opinion of this court that the previous trial of the State of New Jersey versus Charles Jesus Sinclair was rampant with prejudice and egregious wrongdoing and I hereby reverse the sentence of insider trading to one of not guilty. This day of May 23, 1988, you are hereby released from Lewisburg Penitentiary and are free to go."

CJ turned and saw Anna and Shelly with outstretched arms and tears in their eyes. It was a beautiful sight to behold and it would remain in memory for an eternity.

As the three of them cautiously walked down the courthouse steps, CJ looked up to the heavens to acknowledge God for his favors and bounty.

A shiny new blue Cadillac was at the curb waiting to finally take them back home.

A victory celebration was in order and it was to be held at Shelly's home that very evening. All the members of the b.h. conglomerate were present and so was CJ's lifelong friend, O'Neil, who paid for the food and drinks.

Although CJ was glad to see and celebrate with everyone, what he really wanted was a quiet night with his woman and his son. Anticipating CJ's wishes, Mr. Sal announced to all that it was time to leave and let CJ and his family have the remaining night to themselves.

The next day while eating breakfast and playing with his son, CJ called Shelly to join them in the dining room; he had an announcement to make. Shelly came in smiling as usual, and asked: "What is it my dear?"

CJ reached into the pantry closet and retrieved a small package. It was a special gift that he arranged for Sal to pick up when he learned about his possible release from prison. He then asked Shelly to sit for a moment and to please listen. Holding his son by the hand and the package in the other, he walked toward Shelly.

"I have loved you from the first time we met, and even though I didn't know as much then as I do now, my love has increased with each passing day," he said. "I realized when I was incarcerated, more than ever, that God has destined for us to be partners for life.

"My going away was an acid test, to see if you would hold or fold. You came through like a champion and took care of our business, our money, and our son. I am grateful beyond words."

He kneeled before her on one leg and slowly unwrapped the package as Ihsan eagerly looked on, and said:

"When love beckons to you, follow him, though his ways are hard and steep. And when his wings enfold you yield to him," CJ said, quoting the poet Khalil Gibran. He then took a long and deep pause, looked into her beautiful green eyes and said:

"Shelly, I love you and I want you to be my wife, in this life and in the next. Will you marry me?"

He opened the package fully, and presented her with a large and beautiful diamond-studded gold ring. Shelly almost fell from her chair, with tears of joy swelling in those green eyes; she answered the proposal: "Yes! I will marry you and be your loving wife forever and through infinity."

A beautiful June wedding was held at the Tavern on the Green. Shelly looked like Cinderella and CJ was the handsome prince, a lovely couple destined for this day.

The day was complete with relatives and friends, and everyone had a good time. Gifts were plentiful, as were the envelopes filled with cash. It wasn't the money they treasured, however; it was the outpouring of love and well wishes. Mr. Sal gave them a honeymoon in beautiful Hawaii, while Anna and Shelly's dad volunteered to take care of their grandchild until the newlyweds returned.

All was right with the world for now, but there was one pressing thought that still bothered CJ. A few weeks after their return from the honeymoon he discussed it with Shelly. It was the horrific facts he learned concerning the 13th Amendment. He told Shelly he wanted to do something about it, but wasn't sure what.

CJ had compiled information about the cooperation of government and corporations, and their use of prisoners for retail profits. He didn't know how to challenge the status quo or how to inform the public more broadly. The information he discovered about the prison industrial complex was frightening, and he was sure most people were ignorant about it or simply didn't care.

America was the leading culprit in this scheme, he had learned, and jailed more prisoners than any other country on Earth, democratic or otherwise. The highest populations imprisoned were Black and or Hispanic and male. Products made by prisoners' number into the tens of thousands the profits total in multi-billions yearly.

Shelly was very sympathetic and suggested that since they were wealthy and could be completely independent, they become crusaders for prison reform all over the nation. She envisioned a highly sophisticated mechanism that involved print, audio visuals, speaking engagements, and legal activities that would alert and educate the public in an effort to change the current system.

She was always CJ's biggest inspiration and always willing to put their money on the line. Together they set an intention to develop an infrastructure that would tackle this problem head on and attempt to stop the illegal free labor pool and exploitation of poor people under the guise of prison reform.

CJ was approaching the age of 35, and in spite his prison term he believed he had made a positive social /economic impact during his life. He had become a successful accountant, a good financial investor, and had planted a seed in Sal's mind of his dream and hopes of changing the section of town known as the Beehive.

Eighteen months after his release from prison, he was living a moderately comfortable lifestyle in the city of New York, embracing the contentments of marriage and fatherhood. His primary focus was on his freedom and responsibilities in his new environment. He realized that his time was more precious now than ever before, and with the exception of his mother, he gave little time or thought to his former associates or his friends, including his best friend O'Neil.

At the conclusion of his day and daily routine, CJ loved to just relax and witness the broadcasts of nightly news. It was on one such occasion that he saw a story featuring a major construction project about to take place in his old city. As he followed the story, there was a revealing interview about the location of the construction site and the project manager's name. CJ was pleasantly surprised to learn that his longtime friend Sal, with one of his construction companies, was heading up the project.

This news story covered a plan for major restoration and development at one of New Jersey's oldest and now defunct industrial zones. As CJ continued watching he began to recognize that the area being demolished and restored was the Beehive section of his former city.

Shortly after that news, CJ vividly recalled a conversation with Sal when he came to Lewisburg for a visit. Sal spoke at length with CJ of his intentions to buy out the properties within the Beehive section, demolish them, and begin a transformation of the old neighborhood. Sal presented to

CJ a grand-scale vision of redevelopment that would reflect a more modern community. It would feature a broad array of businesses, affordable single-family homes, green space, and some community centers for the youth.

His construction project would result in creating taxable revenue beneficial to the city and the county at-large.

Although these ideas sounded great, somehow CJ hadn't given Sal's plan a serious thought until he witnessed the news story. Sitting in his favorite chair, he was glad when the news went to commercials. A delighted grin came across his face. His heart was pounding as he realized his friend, mentor, and business partner was absolutely serious and that their vision of change had a chance of coming into fruition.

CJ was moved and inspired as a result of this news and immediately shared it with Shelly. Upon hearing about it and the exciting effect it had upon CJ, it was Shelly who suggested a final visit to the infamous Beehive. Shelly desired to bring closure and satisfaction to his heart and reassure him that his sacrifices of imprisonment were not completely in vain. She believed that he had created some good karma and that he was being rewarded by the fulfillment of his dream of transforming that criminalized section of his city into one of respectability.

They concluded that a reunion of the b.h. conglomerate at Dee Dee's Lounge would be the perfect choice.

CJ decided to phone Sal to discuss the possibility of a reunion; after all, CJ hadn't seen anyone since their wedding day. Sal thought it was a great idea because Dee Dee's was scheduled for demolition at a later time and would still be available.

They realized that they were the only two who remained nearby; the other members had relocated beyond the metropolitan area. Sal always remained in touch with the other members and so he began to contact them to discuss a proposed reunion. The reaction was positive and all agreed it was a great idea for one last visit before the transformation of their old stomping ground.

The reunion was scheduled to take place the following spring, allowing enough time for preparation - and because spring is the season that represents fresh life and a new beginning.

The day of the reunion was a beautiful Saturday, with bright sun shining on the smiling faces throughout Dee Dee's Lounge. Everyone was filled with laughter, hugs, and grand stories about good and bad times shared within the Beehive.

CJ gave Shelly a tour of Dee Dee's reminding her of his first visit there with his father. The main reason for the tour was to show her Sal's chess alcove where they played dozens of games.

One area of the lounge was reserved to display a professional, full-scale model and colorful three-dimensional drawings of Sal's vision for the reconstruction project. As people were drawn to this display, they expressed joy and excitement about the way this development would change the scope of this old neighborhood and enhance the overall image of the city.

As the frolicking of old and new patrons continued at Dee Dee's, Sal decided to get everyone's attention for a few words and a toast. CJ was surprised that his longtime friend had beckoned for him to join in at his side.

"Hello, everyone. I want to welcome you all to Dee Dee's Lounge. Please allow me this time for a few short comments. I would first like to thank all of my friends, dignitaries, and former business partners for coming together and attending this well-deserved reunion. It is a special and honorable time whenever one can give back to the community from whence he came. We are here today to celebrate and witness a dream once deferred now being fulfilled.

"I know this may come as a surprise to some of you, but the restoration of the Beehive was a lofty dream initially introduced to me by one of my favorite chess opponents - my friend and protégé. I have always thought of him as the brains and visionary behind any of our concocted schemes, while I and my partners supplied the muscle for seeing them through. I'm asking for everyone to please stand as we salute CJ with a toast and a heartfelt applause."

The cheering, toasting, and applause echoed loudly throughout Dee Dee's Lounge, and it seemed to last forever. All of this was somewhat overwhelming for CJ and he was both embarrassed and moved by Sal's remarks. Throughout his life, CJ was never one to relish attention except from his beloved Shelly. The admiration shown toward CJ made Shelly feel proud as she stood nearly with a smile while loving tears of joy slowly flowed down her tanned cheeks.

"I love you, babe," she loudly proclaimed while blowing kisses at CJ's bashful face. He fondly returned her kisses with, "and I love you more." Throughout the day and before the walking tour of the construction site, which was nearly 50 percent completed, people approached CJ to bestow their appreciation for his years of friendship, accounting skills, marketing insight, and long-term value to his former city.

CJ and Shelly were surprised to see Anna and O'Neil joining the reunion prior to Sal's remarks. The two had planned to meet together as a surprise to CJ and Shelly. Neither of them was going to miss this special occasion.

O'Neil hadn't hung out with CJ in more than a year and Anna hadn't seen many of her friends since the demise of her beloved Carnell. They were aglow from the attention given to CJ as he decided to take the microphone and thank everyone for their outpouring of support and grace.

During his remarks of thanks he mentioned that he and Shelly were thinking of moving from New York and beginning a new residency in the state of Texas. CJ informed the crowd that he'd continue his efforts toward the education, counseling, and exposure of the horrors and entanglements of the prison industrial complex. He said he was determined to engage in whatever was necessary to provide awareness of those dehumanizing institutions. When CJ was a prisoner, his research had rewarded him with the knowledge of enormous monetary gains awarded to whoever owned or controlled prisons - all at the cost of the prisoners losing their citizenship.

The reaction from the gathering about his plans was received positively and many said they would offer money and resources for its success. Anna was surprised and pleased to hear this but she naturally worried about any possible political blowback that might affect her son.

As the participants slowly began leaving, Sal announced that any future reunions would be held at a new Dee Dee's Lounge, which would become an integral part of the overall design of the redevelopment plan.

The b.h. reunion was a successful date to be honored and long remembered by all. It was a love fest and a measurement of how all their lives were changing with time. The registry signed by those in attendance would serve Sal's promise to send pictures documenting the construction progress.

CJ - surrounded by his wife, best friend, and mother - decided to offer their final goodbye hugs and kisses to Sal, Dee Dee, and Artie as they navigated their way toward the door for a safe return home.

As CJ stepped through the doorway, he exhaled into the mild spring night, gazing at the heavens above. He sighed, taking in the dark sky lit by a full moon and brilliant stars. CJ thought this was another sign from God, an omen that all was good with the world, and a new day was coming.

Epilogue

The ride home to New York was filled with laughter and joy, as Shelly and CJ celebrated old friendships and shared their appreciation of new acquaintances. They agreed that it was a wonderful time, mixing with those who had been stable friends in their lives.

Shelly was sure that it did CJ a world of good viewing and talking about the model the drawings and taking in the love that was shown by the community. CJ never had specific ideas about the restoration - he just dreamed that the area could someday be changed to something respectable, and he was pleased that his dream was finally becoming a reality.

It was Sal who possessed the insight and construction knowledge that was making their vision work, and he put together a marvelous team for the restoration of the Beehive.

Shelly and CJ talked about the plans late into the night. They gently put little Ihsan to bed before collapsing into bed themselves with contented minds and joy in their hearts.

During the next three weeks, CJ and Shelly began serious discussions about their relocation to Texas. Neither of them was tired or bored with New York, but they agreed a different pace and environment would benefit the growth and development of their son.

There's no city comparable to New York with its charm, cultural diversity, and worldly lifestyles. There's always something to do in NYC, it's truly the city that never sleeps. The times, however, were changing for both of them and the inner transformation they were experiencing nudged them to think about more relaxed surroundings with an atmosphere of serenity and good old-fashioned Southern hospitality.

CJ also realized that by leaving the New York area he could avoid or lessen the media attention and scrutiny he'd probably receive for his exposure or criticism of prison atrocities and his proposals for reform. New

York City would be available and great for visiting or vacationing; and with Anna residing in New Jersey it would be the perfect place for a getaway.

Shelly happily talked about her growing up in the South with its beautiful country side, horses, and running barefoot through the meadows. Her hair would be flowing against the wind - with laughter - and she was free without a care in the world. She fondly remembered open spaces, an absence of crowds of people, less concrete, and more fresh air, with no skylines - but most of all, friendlier neighbors.

CJ chuckled while struggling to visualize Shelly running barefooted through high grass and wildflowers. He just couldn't imagine her not being the graceful and sophisticated lady he had fallen madly in love with.

Shelly remembered accompanying her dad on business trips, which gave her a familiarity with various parts of the state. She suggested they take a trip and spend time investigating different areas to see what Texas had to offer. They shared a desire to live in a rural or suburban community with enough open space for horses and plenty of room to roam. Neither Shelly nor CJ had a desire to live near the coastlines of Texas. It appeared that a choice of either Fort Worth or Dallas might offer them excellent suburban areas just far enough from urban life.

The spring season was blooming and they realized that now would be the perfect time to inspect prospective properties and homes. Shelly also thought it a good idea to call her dad and get additional input before making any arrangements to visit her home state.

The state of Texas in the middle of springtime is a beautiful sight to behold. Many areas of the state have adopted the theme of "God's Country" as a reminder about its natural beauty and spaciousness.

The trip back home would afford Shelly an opportunity to spend some time with childhood friends and relatives, many of whom hadn't met her new husband, but were anxious to do so.

After a vigorous two-week period of shopping for housing they finally settled on a 7-acre parcel of rolling hills on the outskirts of Fort Worth. It was a magnificent and colorful landscaped property complemented with horse stables, a fishing lake, and a white, two-story Neoclassical Southern-style home.

The home and stables were designed by a premier local architect with a small, young family in mind. It featured a spacious veranda with dramatic, centered columns.

Shelly and CJ appreciated an extra blessing - that they'd be the first family to occupy it. They made a generous offer far above the listing price and signed a contract quickly before making their return to New York.

The progress toward moving seemed to be going well and according to schedule. All that remained now was to put Shelly's condominium on the market for sale. They were confident that could sell it for twice the amount of their new home now awaiting them in Texas, which they did, quickly and uneventfully.

They had made careful arrangements to maintain and control their businesses and investments in New York and Pennsylvania, which were legally secured and left in the capable hands of their experienced and loyal managers.

The spring season was passing and by their calculations they would soon be spending their first full summer in the comfort of their new Texas home.

After much anticipation by the Sinclair family, moving day finally arrived. The trucks were all loaded and ready for the journey to Texas. Shelly, CJ, and Ihsan happily waved to the drivers, wishing them a safe journey and Godspeed.

Moving day was special for another reason: Anna and O'Neil had booked reservations for the Sinclair family at Tavern on the Green. It was an evocative location for Shelly and CJ because it held romantic memories of their first date and had become their most favorite restaurant in all of Manhattan.

On moving day, they gathered together as one family to dine, drink, and be merry one more time before saying goodbyes and parting.

"You take care of my boys," said Anna with tears of sadness and joy streaming down her face.

"Are you kidding," replied Shelly, "They are my inspiration and reason for living; in fact they are the air I breathe."

"Hey, man," said O'Neil, "you keep me informed about the single, rich ladies down there. I don't want to travel that far for nothing."

"Are you seriously ready to settle down with just one?" CJ asked.

"No," replied O'Neil; "not yet. I just want to make that journey worth my while."

Everyone laughed, hugged, and shed tears before the new Sinclair family headed to the boarding gate, blowing kisses and waving goodbyes.

The sunsets in Texas are beautiful and it was setting on an old chapter of their lives.

In the morning a sunrise would follow and shine light on a new chapter. Shelly's heart was full of contentment as she returned to her homeland. She looked forward to caring for the two men in her life in the serene new home they shared.

CJ was also content and determined to focus helping the helpless in cooperation with his powerful friends. He and Shelly had acquired enough wealth to aid them in any legal expenses that would result from their campaign for prison reform. He was embracing the reality of life being short, and he wanted to love his family and be loved in return by his family as his father did before him.

Shelly and CJ were settling into the comfort of their new home and southern environment. They were optimistically looking forward to sharing spiritual and humanitarian values that would promote love far beyond their home and help create a redeeming lifestyle.

As they stood on the second-floor balcony overlooking the landscape, CJ envisioned exploring with his son some of the things that weren't available in his youth. He thought of fishing, horseback riding, and maybe even hunting; however, he still loved playing chess.

Ihsan was 4 years old now and showing clear signs of wit and intelligence. At the end of the day, with his son sitting in his lap, CJ would explain the moves of the game that taught him to think strategically in business and in life.

"This is a knight and it moves this way and that way," he would say.

Or, "The game is over, son. And that's what you call checkmate.

The end

Printed in the United States
By Bookmasters